Follow Author Andre Ray on Social Media

Facebook/Amazon

www.facebook.com/Author.AndreRay

www.Amazon.com/author/andreray

Author of Undercover Deacon

Other books by Author Andre Ray

Undercover Deacon

Http://www.amazon.com/dp/B01AYOPH3G/

Undercover Deacon 2

Http://www.amazon.com/dp/B01AYSPS6S/

Never Letting Go

HTTP://www.amazon.com/dp/B01G12CMP6

Temptation Has A Price

Http://www.amazon.com/dp/B01CQ3OLQC/

Serenity Through The Storm

HTTP://www.amazon.com/dp/B01IS4FCFW

ACKNOWLEDGEMENTS

I would like to express my sincere appreciation to the following people. Without their help, this book would not have been possible.

First and foremost, my Savior Jesus Christ, and the Holy Spirit for giving me inspiration to minister this message.

I want to especially thank my lovely wife and family. Without your love and prayers to keep me going, this road couldn't be traveled. You are truly my rock in every season of my life.

I also want to thank my wonderful editor, Maryam Fakhradeen. Your guidance and critical eye are second to none.

Last but not least, I want to thank the readers of Christian Fiction. Without each one of you, this would not be possible. I pray that my books are a source of inspiration and hope for all

Contents

I walked into Faith of Abundance Church of God in downtown Atlanta on Sunday morning like any other day to enjoy a wonderful service. At that time, I had no way of knowing that when it was over, my life would never be the same. I took my seat in the middle row as I always do. The service was packed which was normal for a church this size with over 3,400 members. The Praise Team was just wrapping up and walking off as Pastor Jerome Blake was stepping up to address the congregation. He's one of the oldest pastors in this area. He stands around 5'8 with gray hair. He has these hazel eyes that make you want to confess all your sins when he looks at you through his thick glasses. He always tells us that he used to play semi-pro basketball, but I just laugh when he starts rubbing his oversized belly while preaching. I reached into my purse to ensure my cell phone was on vibrate mode. Why is this young man sitting beside me watching my every move? He's starting to worry me. I looked around for an empty seat, so I could move before I tell him off but there was none.

I placed my things down under my seat crossing my legs while positioning myself toward the sister sitting beside me. Hopefully this gesture would be enough for him to get the message that I didn't want to be bothered. I turned my head and acted like I was waving to someone in the row across from us, so I could get a better look at this brown-skinned stranger sitting beside me. He was well dressed, I must say, in his brown double-breasted suit and matching tie. He looks to be around 27 or 29 years old with black wavy hair. His eyes were hazel like Pastor Blake's, but I know he doesn't have a son. Alright, lady, get a hold of yourself because the house of the Lord is no place for the thoughts running through your mind right now. I resumed my position while asking the Holy Spirit to keep my mind in check. Pastor Blake was talking but I didn't hear what he was saying. Everyone was standing up so I rose up like I knew what was going on.

"Let us bow our heads in prayer. Father, we thank you for allowing us to come together once again as believers of your Word. Fill us with your Holy Spirit which keeps our minds and bodies in perfect peace. Father, we pray for those that are hurting and in need of healing. Help me to deliver a message that will edify your people. In Jesus' name, amen. Now, before you are seated, turn to your neighbor and see if there is a prayer request that they may be in need of."

What did this man just say? Turn to your neighbor? Lord, give me strength. It felt like everything went in slow motion as I tried to move myself in that direction. I wanted to pray with the sister sitting next to me, but she was already holding hands with the person next to her. When I turned to face this stranger I had to look up because he was around 6'8. He reached down taking my hands and started to speak.

"Sister, my name is Malachi. Do you have a prayer request this morning?"

Do I have a prayer request he wants to know. Only request I have right now is for the Lord to give me back five years in age. I didn't know what to say, but I was glad I decided to wear my good Brazilian wig this morning.

"Good morning, my name is Sister Sandra Washington. Please pray for me to have more strength in my Christian walk. Do you have a prayer request?"

"Well, Sister Sandra Washington, pleasure to meet you this morning. My request is to know what God's will is for my life."

As he was talking, his deep James Earl Jones voice had my whole body vibrating. While praying for each other I couldn't help but notice his Dolce & Gabbana cologne which filled the air around us. By his prayer request I'm not sure if he is even saved, but I'm not going to make any quick judgments. Holding hands we closed our eyes and began to pray for each other. A few minutes later, Pastor Blake asked for everyone to be seated as the choir was preparing to sing. I took my seat again, but this time I crossed my legs toward his direction. I wonder if he even knows what this action means in body language. My focus should be on the choir and getting into the presence of the Lord. Instead, I find myself drifting my eyes over to where he is sitting.

I managed to pull it together by standing, and forcing myself to get into the song the Praise Team was singing.

Just when I was getting him out of my head they ended their song. I could just continue to stand here and wait until Pastor Blake comes up which would buy me more time. Wait. That's Elder Kent coming up to speak.

"Good morning, people of God. Everyone please take your seats for a few quick announcements."

Are you kidding me right now? Just when I was back where I needed to be spiritually? Ok Sandra, you can do this. Just sit down and keep your eyes forward. All is well.

"Excuse me, I think you dropped this."

Ok girl, don't look him in the eyes. Just reach your hand out and let him place whatever it is in there. Nothing is happening. What is he waiting for? He's forcing me to look so he can take me back to that place I fought so hard to escape. "Devil, get thee behind me," I said as I turned my head. It was the program the Ushers were handing out as we came inside.

"Thank you, Malachi. You are so kind."

"It was my pleasure, Sandra," he said with a smile.

Great. Now my program smells just like him. The devil is not making this easy at all. Elder Kent, will you sit your behind down so Pastor can start preaching? So I can get some Word.

"That will be all the announcements this morning. Now, this next man needs no introduction but stand and help me to welcome our very own, Pastor Blake."

"Thank you, please be seated as our first-time visitors remain standing, so we can welcome you to our congregation this morning."

Ok, why isn't he sitting down with the rest of us? Don't jump to conclusions, he may be visiting because his church is not having service or he has family here. I looked around to see who he could be with because that Sister Dean is always trying to show off her family when they come into town. I'll just wait until after service and see who he talks to. Then, I'll know more about this stranger who has somehow captured my attention. I need the Pastor to let them sit now.

"Members of Faith of Abundance Church of God, as the Praise Team sings our welcome song, please stand and greet our first-time visitors."

"Sandra, they have a wonderful way of making first-time visitors feel welcomed. I see you didn't stand up. You must be a member here."

"Yes we do. I've been here for years now."

Thank you, Lord, for giving me an opening to this mystery man. "I take it you are new to the area."

"No, just always wanted to come hear one of Pastor Blake's messages in person."

Only thing his answer did was leave me with more questions. At least he brought a Bible with him. I already checked the condition of his nails to see what type of work he could be doing. I don't have time to babysit another broke man. This is all a little too much for me right now; I need to go to the ladies room. Which way do I get up and leave? If I go by him then I have to decide which way to face my body leaving me exposed either way. If I exit from the other side, he may think I'm trying to avoid him. Wow, all this from just turning to your neighbor. I want to have a long talk with the person who started this. All these years of being saved and filled with the Holy Spirit and I'm allowing myself to become weak. Am I still a work in progress? Well, here goes nothing...

I stood up, holding my purse in front of me while working my way passed him. Being the perfect gentleman he turned his head. As I made my way toward the doors, I noticed Sister Dean giving me that look of hers. This made me wonder again if he could be part of her family.

Walking into the ladies room, I placed my purse on the counter taking a long look into the mirror. I came face-to-face with a 45, 5'7, brown eyes and skin, and long brown hair, which is my favorite wig, woman. This is the house of the Lord, but I'm standing in the bathroom all caught up in my feelings for some man I don't even know. Well, Sister Sandra Washington, you are a woman of God and a highly respected person in the community. Pull yourself together before you allow the devil to take you down a road you can't get off of. I wanted to throw some cold water on my face, but I would have to redo my makeup. Carefully wiping the small tear drop from the corner of my right eye, I made my way back to the service.

"I hope everything is alright, Sister?"

"Everything is fine. I just needed to use the ladies' room."

Well, I can say for a young man he sure does have great manners. Now, let me get and keep my attention on the preaching of Pastor Blake.

"Brothers and Sisters, this morning I want to talk to you about keeping your mind off the call of the flesh."

"Am I getting punked right now by the Holy Spirit?" I said while looking around.

"This is a calling that we all, including myself, have to deal with on a daily basis. The notion of the flesh is other than the mind, is the biggest battle a Christian will have to face, whether you tell the truth or not. You can try and hide when you feel weak in the flesh, but time uncovers all sins done in the dark. The temptation does not come in the form we want it, but it will come in the form of a well-dressed spirit."

"Pastor Blake, get out of my head. Amen to that though; mine is sitting right beside me," I said to myself, cutting my eyes over at Malachi.

"It could attack you anywhere on any given day. Even in the house of the Lord because brick and mortar alone will not keep the devil out. You need to be rooted and grounded in the Word of the Lord, but more importantly, you have to be living it daily. Turn in your Bibles to Ephesians 6:12-13. It reads: **For we wrestle not against flesh and blood, but against principalities, against powers, against the rulers of the darkness of this world, against spiritual wickedness in high places. Wherefore take unto you the whole armor of God, that ye may be able to withstand in the evil day, and having done all, to stand.** Now, turn to your neighbor and say: I have on my full armor of God, and my flesh is under control."

Again the sister sitting next to me had already turned to the person who was sitting beside her, leaving me no other option. Malachi was staring into my eyes with this look that made my armor crack right down the middle. I couldn't even get my mouth open to say the words so I just listened as he repeated what Pastor said.

"I have on my full armor of God, and my flesh is under control," is what he said, but this is what my flesh heard: "I'm going to tear your armor off and take you unto myself."

"Lord, if Pastor Blake don't end this service soon, you are going to lose another one," I said to myself while turning to face the front.

"Let us keep each other in prayer as we leave this place. Everyone please stand as we close out in prayer. Father, as we leave this place, keep us in perfect peace. Don't let the tricks of the devil penetrate the armor you have given us. In Jesus' name, amen. Hug someone before you leave, and go in peace, people of God."

He just won't stop with this hugging thing. This time I reached for the sister before she even had a chance to move. I know she had to be wondering why I was hugging her so hard, but if she could read minds she would understand. I picked up my purse and Bible and followed her out so I didn't have to make eye contact with Malachi. The way he has me right now I may have to look for another service to attend. I heard him calling my name but I kept it moving. Making it to my car, I just tossed my purse and Bible into the passenger seat then adjusted the rearview mirror to where I could see myself.

"What in the world just happen in there this morning?" I said out loud while trying to get my emotions together.

Whoever this man is has got me all caught up in my feelings right now. Pulling up my center armrest, I took out my small bottle of hand sanitizer pouring some onto my hands trying to eliminate the smell of his cologne that was still lingering which was not helping matters. Putting in one of my Worship CD's to keep my mind from wandering to where it didn't need to be right now, I waited for an opening to pull into line to exit the parking lot.

Chapter 2

I had planned to drive over to Lenox Square to get this dress I saw on sale the other day, but the way I'm feeling right now I just need to head to the house. I pulled up to my townhouse located in the beautiful community of Alexandria. Parking my BMW in the garage, I was ready to get out of these church clothes and settle in for the rest of the day. Just as I was getting out of the car I heard a man's voice calling my name. I turned around dropping my purse on the ground while freezing in my tracks.

"Hello, Sister Washington. I didn't know you stayed in my neighborhood. Good to see you again."

It was Malachi sitting in a white Lexus. This day is getting stranger by the hour. Come on and pull yourself together before this man thinks something is wrong with you.

"It's good to see you again too. I just moved in last week. I'm in the process of selling my other house across town, but I like it here better; feels more like home to me."

"I see you dropped your purse, hope I didn't startle you. Do you need a hand picking it up?"

"I'm good, just clumsy is all. Which house do you stay in if you don't mind me asking?"

"Not at all. I would be upset if you didn't. I stay just around the corner, so if you ever need anything just let me know. Well, I have a couple of steaks that need seasoning for tonight's dinner calling my name, so I should be heading home. See you around the neighborhood," he said pulling off.

Picking up my purse from the ground I couldn't help but smile. Just imagining him cooking has me all...let me get my behind in the house before I backslide myself into hell. Setting my things down on the table, I couldn't help but think how he didn't mention which home was his. Walking into the bedroom, I tossed my Christian Louboutin heels to the side while taking a seat on the bed. As I sat there, I tried to piece today's events together. What I need now is a long shower because this Atlanta heat has my body all sticky. I made my way into the bathroom after I laid an outfit on the bed to change into.

After about 30 minutes I turned the water off and dried off. Once I was dressed, I went into the kitchen to see what I could fix for dinner that wouldn't take up too much time. Since I'm single I don't keep a lot of food in the house so it won't go to waste. From what I see here, it looks like it's going to be another salad and red wine night. It was still early so I curled up on the sofa to take a short nap. I couldn't have been more than a few hours into my nap when I heard the front doorbell ring. This is a gated community and I know I wasn't expecting guests today. When I looked through the peephole, all I saw was a huge chest. Who in the world could this be?

"Yes, can I help you with something?"

"Sister Washington, its Malachi. I hope I didn't come at a bad time."

"Just give me a second, please."

What in the world is he doing back here already? I know I didn't give him any indication that something could happen between us. Wait. I'm getting ahead of myself. Let's see what he wants first. Alright, let's do a quick check of things and myself before I open this door.

When I opened the door he was standing there holding a large food basket. He was dressed in black slacks, black shoes, and a pressed purple shirt which was unbuttoned enough to expose his chest.

"Well, hello. I didn't expect to see you again so soon. To what do I owe the pleasure of this visit?"

"I was making dinner when I thought to myself: why should I be the only one enjoying this delicious steak? So, I made enough for two. I hope you haven't eaten anything yet."

"This is more than anything I expected on this Sunday evening. You definitely have me at a loss for words right now. Please, come in and give your hands a rest. You can set everything down in the kitchen. I didn't take you for the cooking type, Malachi."

"When you live alone you learn a lot in a short period of time. I hope you like you steak mid-well."

"I normally don't partake in other people's cooking when I don't know them, but this looks like it was prepared by a professional chef. I see you even brought a bottle of wine."

"Well, I think red wine goes great with a good wagyu ribeye."

"A man of good taste I see. This is $100 per pound. Guess I won't have to cook tonight."

"Sister Washington, I hope the bottle of wine is not overstepping your beliefs."

"Please, call me Sandra. When you say it like that I feel like someone's grandmother. I do have a glass in moderation."

"Well, Sandra shall we take a seat before everything gets cold, and get to know each other a little better. Do you have a corkscrew?"

"Yes, let me get it out of the kitchen. I'll be right back."

"I'll be right here waiting," he said laughing.

Walking into the kitchen, I dipped out of his view so I could catch up with my feelings.

"Sandra Washington, what are you doing, lady?" I said in a low voice while holding onto the countertop with both hands.

All I can do right now is pray for strength, so I made my way back into the dining room.

"Here we go. Hope I didn't keep you waiting."

"Here, let me pull out your chair and pour you the first glass."

"Thank you, sir. You are again, the perfect gentleman. So, Malachi what did you say you do for a living?"

"I don't remember saying anything about it, but I'm into the financial market."

"That is something because I'm a loan officer at a bank. Isn't that a coincidence?"

"Why yes it is. Look, let's not talk shop right now. I want to get to know who Sandra Washington really is."

"There isn't much to tell. I'm an Atlanta girl born and bred, educated at the finest schools money could buy and I've been divorced for two years now. Maybe that last part was a little more information then I needed to share."

"I'm sorry your marriage didn't work out, but it looks like you pulled yourself together well."

"It was hard at first but my faith in God helped me through the worst days. Enough about that, tell me about yourself and why you are really here. I'm sure you have better places to be and ladies your own age you could be spending your time with."

"Well, being only 27 years old there isn't much of my life story to tell. My current work status you already know. I moved out here last year as a gift to myself when I landed my job. I'm currently an eligible bachelor, and what brought me to your door was intrigue."

"What can be so intriguing about me? I'm old enough to be your mother even though I don't look like it."

"No, you don't that is for sure. I feel like age is just a number as long as you don't go too low.

I find that a seasoned woman makes for a better teacher of life."

"What could I possibly teach a young man with an already smooth persona?"

"Can I pour you another glass of wine, my lady?" he said with a smile.

"See what I mean. You smoothly changed the subject just like that. Nice touch, Malachi. What is your last name away?"

"It's Steel. I'm sorry for not telling you before now."

"It's fine. This wine is starting to get to me a little. I'm not too much of a drinker."

"Would you like another glass?" he said picking up the bottle.

I placed my hand over my glass. I've been out the game for a minute, but I knew what he was trying to do. "Pump your breaks, Mr. Steel. I think it is best we end this meal right here. Thank you for dinner, but I have to get ready for a long day at work tomorrow. I'll show you to the front door."

"I hope I didn't say or do anything out of line. Maybe we can have lunch one day this week?"

"Let's just leave it right here for now because I don't want you getting any wrong ideas. Have a good night, Mr. Steel."

"You too, Ms. Washington," he said as I closed the door.

"Lord, I hope you didn't send this young man into my life because I don't know if I can handle this one," I prayed as I was taking the dishes into the kitchen. Once I had everything done, I made my way upstairs to get ready for the dreaded day I hate the most: Monday. This sure has been a Sunday though.

I awoke the next day still feeling the effects of the wine from last night. "I guess my age is starting to show," I said, laughing while making my way into the bathroom.

Once I was dressed and I'd grabbed my morning coffee, I made my way to the car. What is this on my windshield? The garage door was down so how anyone could have gotten in is a mystery. It was a single red rose and a card.

After checking for any damage I carefully removed them. The rose gave off a lovely scent, and the card read:

"Good morning, Sandra. I just wanted to start your day off with a smile. Malachi."

Well, he did accomplish his mission even though someone being inside my garage doesn't make me too happy. Guess I'll be setting the alarm more often now. I still forgot to ask him if he was even saved. Again, why am I stressing over a young man I don't even know? I placed the card and rose on the passenger seat and started heading to the downtown area of Atlanta, where my job was located. Getting through this traffic is like playing Russian roulette. I kept glancing over to look at the red rose, wondering what effect he would have if I lowered the walls I've built and allow him into my life.

I pulled up to Fidelity Bank looking through the windows before heading to the parking garage as I have done for six years.

"Good morning, Ms. Washington. I see you had a great weekend."

"Just a little something from a new friend to brighten my morning," I replied with a smile.

"Well, I guess you have two friends because someone sent you roses this morning. I placed them on your desk already."

"Thank you, Lisa. Not sure who could have sent them."

Walking into my office going straight for the card that was attached, I wanted to know who this could be. It read:

"Sandra, I hope theses roses still find you with a smile on your face like the first one did. Malachi."

"Lisa, did a delivery person bring these, and what did he look like?"

"Yes, it was a female and she was white with short red hair..."

"Alright, that's all I needed to know. Thank you, Lisa."

"I hope everything is alright, Ms. Washington. I didn't do anything wrong did I?"

"Of course not Lisa. It's just that this past weekend had more excitement than I'm accustomed to. Hold my calls for about an hour."

"Yes, Ms. Washington. You don't have anything pressing for this morning."

I walked into my office placing the single rose back with the others as a big smile came over my face. Walking around to take a seat in the brown leather chair, I leaned back while turning it to stare out the window. I was feeling all kinds of emotions that had been locked away since my last marriage. Wait. What in the world am I doing sitting here, getting all caught up with Malachi like he's my man? "Sandra, get a hold of yourself," I said getting up and picking up the roses.

"Lisa, please place these somewhere in the sitting area so the customers will have something pretty to look at when they come in today."

"I thought you were happy about getting these, Ms. Washington."

"Lisa, will you just do like I asked, please?"

I went back into my office slamming the door. Sitting back down at my desk, I punched in my password and pulled up my emails. When they came up, I just sat there staring at the screen with my mouth open in disbelief. Somehow Malachi sent me over 30 emails. I never gave him my email address, so how could this be on my computer? What in the world is he up to I wonder. After reading the first one, I just deleted the rest without opening them. While going over some loan requests my phone started to ring.

"Good morning, this is Ms. Washington."

"Good morning, I hope the roses brightened your morning."

"Malachi, your gesture this morning was very sweet, but I can't accept gifts of that nature from you. I hope you didn't get the wrong impression from dinner."

"Sandra, I sent the roses to you hoping to gain nothing more than a smile upon your face on a Monday. I know how Mondays can be for us professionals. If you got anything other than that, I apologize."

"Well, I guess I just made a fool of myself."

"Not everything is what it appears, Ms. Washington. My feelings are truly hurt."

"Please forgive me, Malachi. How can I make this up to you?"

"How about lunch this afternoon?"

"I'm in no position to say no right now. Just say when and where."

"I can come and pick you up from the bank around noon then we can decide together on a location."

"Malachi, I don't think that will be a good idea because people here love to gossip. I'll meet you wherever you like."

"Understand that. Let's meet at Aviva by Kameel if you don't mind Mediterranean food."

"That will work for me. Guess I'll see you for lunch then. I'm sorry, but I really need to get some loans processed now, so..."

"Of course. Goodbye, Sandra."

Placing the receiver back down, it hit me that I forgot to inquire how he got into my garage this morning. No matter; I will put an end to all this today. I'm too old for this foolishness.

Chapter 3

"Ms. Washington, you asked me to remind you when it was getting close to noon."

"Thank you, Lisa. Alright, Mr. and Mrs. Jones, I think I have everything I need to process your loan application. You should hear something from the bank in about a week. Thank you for coming in today."

"Thank you, Ms. Washington. We sure hope this goes through because we'd like to open our business this fall."

After walking them to the door, I retrieved my purse then headed to the restaurant. I checked my watch before going inside because I didn't want to seem anxious. Looking around, I spotted him sitting at a table by the wall. He was looking sharp in his tan double-breasted suit and white shirt with matching tie.

"Good afternoon, Mr. Steel."

"Hello, I didn't see you come up. Allow me to pull out your seat."

"Thank you for picking some place close. I hate driving in lunchtime traffic. Shall we go up and get something to eat?"

"Yes, let me leave my jacket so no one takes our seats."

I let him lead the way so I didn't have to worry about him staring at my behind. Once we both had got our plates we returned to the table. I looked around hoping no one from the church was here today. Last thing I need is for that Sister Dean to have something to run her mouth about.

"Thanks again, Sandra for joining me for lunch. You are looking good in that blue dress."

"Malachi, I need to get something off my chest before we get too far into this conversation."

"Wow. I feel like this is a breakup lunch date," he said leaning back in his seat.

"Your reaction and statement is conformation I need to do this. Malachi, I feel like we just need to keep our distance from each other after today because you are seeing something that is not there or that could never happen."

"Well, I didn't expect this. Sandra, let me save you some time and just leave right now."

"Wait. Malachi, I didn't want this to happen."

"Save your breath, Ms. Washington. You don't have to worry about seeing me again."

He just walked off before I could get another word out my mouth. The look on his face told me he was not happy at all with my statement. I just sat back down and continued to eat my meal because I wasn't about to let this ruin my afternoon. Once I was done, I made my way back to the office.

"Welcome back, Ms. Washington."

"Lisa, where are the roses that you put in the lobby?"

"Some fine looking gentleman came in and took them about 20 minutes ago. I didn't stop him because I assumed you knew about it."

"I didn't authorize such a thing but it will be fine. Hold my calls until I tell you different, Lisa."

"Yes, Ms. Washington."

I stormed into my office slamming the door behind me. Tossing my purse on the desk I picked up the phone to give Malachi a call.

"Malachi, I'm not surprised that you let your phone go to voicemail considering the way you left the restaurant. Don't you ever come to my job and remove anything again. I'm not one of your young lady friends that you can play silly games with, and be sure to lose my number along with my address. Goodbye!!"

"Sandra, is everything alright in here? I can hear you clear across the hallway."

"Sorry about that, Mr. Jones. I was just a little upset with someone."

"This is a business, Ms. Washington, and not a place for your personal shenanigans. Let's keep it professional, alright?"

"Yes, sir. I completely understand, and it won't happen again."

I had known idea the president of the back was going to be here today. This thing with Malachi is affecting my life which I didn't see coming from just one church service. I truly need to be more careful about who I pray with from now on because some people get caught up in their feelings real quick. I managed to get back to work and get everything caught up.

"Ms. Washington, its 5:30. I'm on my way out if you don't need anything else."

"No, I'll be right behind you in about 10 minutes. Lisa, I apologize if I was in any way short with you today."

"It's fine. I know you been under pressure with things lately. Have a good night."

"Have a good night, Lisa."

When I was done with the last of what I was doing I made my way to the parking garage. I was so ready for a nice glass of wine, and the chance to put this day behind me.

"Sandra, can I talk to you for a second?"

"Malachi, what in the world are you doing here?! You scared me to death."

"Look, I'm not trying to cause you any problems. I just wanted to apologize for my actions at lunch."

"This is not the time and place. You lucky I didn't shoot your behind because I'm always packing and don't forget that. Now, move out my way so I can be on my way."

"Sandra, I just want to talk to you, please."

"You must be crazy if you think I'm going to stand here in a parking garage and talk to you about anything. Do I need to call the police?" I said pulling out my cell phone.

He just put his hands in the air and started walking backwards. "No need for all that. I'll let you have your space for now."

I jumped into my car trying to push the start button with my shaking hand. Putting the car in drive, I pressed the gas pedal all the way to the floorboard. Good thing I always back in when parking. I drove straight home, and made sure all of the window and doors were locked. Placing my handgun on the kitchen countertop, I poured me a glass of red wine to settle my nerves. If that fools comes around here I will defend myself, believe that. I jumped when I heard something in the other room. Let me get my Bible and do some praying before I lose my mind.

"Lord, I need you to take over this situation. I don't know what or how this man has chosen me to come after, but I need him to just leave me alone. Father, I put my trust in you, amen."

After praying, I fixed myself some dinner and took it into the living room. While watching the television I kept hearing something hitting against the front door. With everything that happened today I wasn't about to go see what it was. I picked up my cell phone and dialed 9-1-1.

"9-1-1. What is your emergency?"

"This is Sandra Washington. I think someone is outside my front door trying to get inside."

"What is your address, Ms. Washington?"

"3127 Lenox Rd. Please hurry!"

"Stay calm, I have units dispatched to your location now."

"It's getting louder! They are trying to break down the front door. Help me, please!!"

"Units in route to 3127 Lenox Rd., be advised the caller said the suspect is trying to break down the front door. All units responding step up your response to code three."

"132 and all units on scene at 3127 Lenox Rd."

"Ms. Washington, units are on scene at your residence now. Please go to the front door."

I dropped the phone rushing to the front door. "Who is out there!?" I yelled through the door.

"This is the Atlanta Sheriff's Office, Ms. Washington."

"Thank the Lord. Did you catch him?"

"Ms. Washington, I'm Sargent Lynn. I have deputies checking the area, but the only thing I found at your front door was this little guy. Does he belong to you?"

"I feel like a fool for calling you now. This is the next door neighbor's dog."

"That is what we are here for, but it had to be something else going on to make you call."

"Nothing I can think of right now, I just heard a noise outside my door that's all. Thank you for coming."

"Well, if you think of what it was don't hesitate to give us a call. Enjoy your night, Ms. Washington."

I watched as he walked back to his patrol car then drove off. I couldn't tell him about Malachi because that would show what a fool I've been.

After relocking the door and making sure again that the rest were secured, I went up to get ready for bed. It was early but I had enough for today. Once I took my shower I remembered my glass of wine was still sitting on the end table in the living room. I walked back down to retrieve it. On the way back up the stairs I heard that same knocking sound at the front door. It has got to be that dog. Turning around, I went back down.

"Dog, if you don't get your little self away from my front door!" I said opening the door.

"Hello, Sandra. Did you miss me?"

I just stood there with my mouth wide open.

"What's the matter, cat got your tongue? You really didn't think I was that easy to get rid of did you?"

"Malachi, what are you doing here? I thought we had an understanding that I didn't want you in my life. Now, please leave my house before I call the police back."

"Go right ahead if you like because I didn't hear you tell them about me the first time they showed up, so I'm sure my name want come up."

"What is it that you want from me, Malachi? I'm not going to stand here and play these games with you."

"All you had to do was stand there and hear me out in the parking garage then we wouldn't be doing this."

"Doing what, Malachi? You must be on some type of medication or drugs because the words coming out of your mouth are stupid."

"Look at you calling yourself a Christian and standing there judging me when all this has been of your own doing. I treated you with nothing but kindness and in return look how you have shown the love of Jesus. I'll leave and you can go back to your perfect life."

I may hate myself for this later. "Wait. I'm sorry for the way I treated you, Malachi. Being a Christian I should know better. Please come inside and let's talk."

"Are you sure this time and not going to slam the door in my face when I get there?"

"I'm sure. Now please get yourself in here."

Lord, I hope this is not going to be one of those decisions I will regret for the rest of my life.

Chapter 4

We went into the living room taking a seat on the sofa. I just sat there staring at him looking at my legs protruding from my nightgown. I tried my best to cover up but I left my robe upstairs. Maybe this wasn't the smartest thing I've done today. I went to stand up so I could walk him back to the door when out of nowhere he began to cry like a baby.

"Malachi, is everything alright with you?"

"I'll be fine just give me a second please. I was just thinking of my mother and how she wanted me to find that person who would be everything the Lord has for me."

"You said wanted. Is your mother still alive?"

"I wish she was, but she passed away a few years ago. It's been so hard on me."

Laughter filled the air. "Look at me sitting in your home crying like a little child. Please forgive me, Sandra."

"I judged you falsely when all you wanted to do was show me what a deep, caring person you are. I love a man who wears his heart on his sleeve; especially one who loves his mother."

"Thanks for understanding. I never meant you any ill will. Can we somehow start over?"

"Of course we can. How about we try lunch again tomorrow?"

"I would like that a lot. Where would you like to meet?"

"How about we meet around 12:30 at Empire State South restaurant?"

"Sounds great, now let me get out of your space so you can get some sleep."

"Yes, this has been an eventful night to say the least, but I'm glad we cleared things up. Have a wonderful evening, Malachi."

I walked him to the door and waited until he was out of sight before closing the door. While walking up the stairs I couldn't help but to recall what the Bible says about judging others. If I had gotten that young man locked up for nothing, which happens every day, it would have weighed on my spirit for a long time. I have to stop letting my bad marriage affect the way I see other men. Who knows this could be the blessing I need. But look at me just rambling away; I'm off to bed.

The next morning when I woke up something felt different in my spirit, but I wasn't sure what it was. Brushing it off I went into the bathroom to get ready for work. When I stepped out of the shower I could hear my cell phone ringing. "Who could be calling me this early in the morning?" I said wrapping the towel around myself while walking over to pick it up. The call was coming from a blocked number.

"Hello? Who is this?" I answered.

"Be very careful of who you let into your life. Consider this a warning."

"Who in the world is this?!" I shouted into the phone holding it up to my mouth.

"Howard, this better not be you playing on my darn phone." The caller hung up without saying another word.

I know he is not trying to start his mess up again after all this time. That is why I divorced his crazy behind in the first place. He must still be riding by here trying to see who I'm dating. Why can't people just let you live your life after they didn't want to be married in the first place? Tossing it on the bed, I went back to get ready.

I went downstairs into the kitchen to grab my morning coffee before heading out the door. When I got to the car I was kind of down. I did not find a single rose on the windshield today. If you start something with a woman you better be sure you can keep it going because we love consistency. On the drive into work I popped in a Marvin Sapp CD to get my praise and worship on. This may be old to some, but to me it's my life in a nutshell. "Let's go Marvin," I said singing alone:

>*"Never would have made it;*
>
>*Never could have made it, without you;*
>
>*I would have lost it all, but now I see how you were there for me;*

And I can say, never would have made it;

Never could have made it, without you;

I would have lost it all, but now I see how you were there for me and I can say;

I'm stronger, I'm wiser, I'm better, much better..."

A car horn blows out of nowhere. "Look lady, I'm glad you made it. How about staying in your lane so the rest of us can make it too," some guy in the car next to me shouted.

I couldn't do nothing but laugh because I was all in his lane, but Marvin will have you all over the place caught up in worship. After parking and walking into the bank I realized that I forgot to stop and look inside. This thing with Malachi is throwing me off my routine, and that strange phone call didn't help any.

"Good morning, Ms. Washington. Hope your day is going better than yesterday."

"Morning, Lisa. Let's just see how things progress shall we?"

I went into my office and jumped right into loan applications. Around 10:30 I started getting this vibe like something was going to happen but I couldn't for the life of me know what it could be.

"Sir, you can't just walk into her office without an appointment."

"I think I can see my wife when I want to thank you."

I looked up to see what was going on. It was Howard standing in the doorway. He is 52, 5'8, medium build, bald with glasses. Nothing to write home about, so whatever did I see in him?

"Howard, what are you doing here in my office?"

"Ms. Washington, do I need to call the police?"

"Its fine, Lisa, I can handle Mr. Carson just fine."

"Sandra, why are you making a fool of yourself going around with that young man?"

"Who I go out with is none of your business anymore. Maybe if you thought about that and kept your mess in your pants we would not be standing here having this conversation."

"Look, I know I messed up. I'm owning that now, but I still love you, and I'm concerned about your safety. He is way too young for you, can't you see that?"

"All I see is you standing in my office acting like a fool. It is way too late for you to act like you care for me now. Please leave before I have the police come escort you off the property."

"There is no need for all that. I'll leave but you just remember what I said about how everything is not always what it seems."

"Whatever, Howard; I don't need your sudden concern. Especially not from someone who fooled me for years. Goodbye."

He left and I got back to work. I couldn't believe the nerve of him trying to still control my life after what he's done. A few hours later, I headed off to lunch.

I drove over to the restaurant to meet up with Malachi. When I walked in he was easy to spot wearing a gray suit, purple shirt, shoes, and tie; all matching. He looked like he just came from a photo shoot which had me a little weak in the knees. I walked over placing my hand on his shoulder.

"Hello, Sandra. I came a little early so we could get a good seat. How is your day going?"

"I don't care to talk about that if you don't mind."

"Someone has upset you, and I want to be here for you."

"You are too sweet. It was my ex-husband. First, he calls me trying to warn me, and then he came by my job a few hours ago with the same nonsense."

"What could he have to warn you about so badly to go through so much trouble?"

"He wanted to warn me about seeing you, Malachi. Please tell me now if there is anything to be concerned about."

"Sandra, I don't know what he has told you, but I'm as safe to be around as a newborn baby."

"That's good enough for me, but you don't feel our age difference affects anything?"

"I didn't notice there was a difference until you just brought it up, Sandra."

"The perfect comeback; I didn't think it mattered either."

We both just sat there and stared each other down for a minute until the waitress came over to the table. We laughed it off then ordered our food. After talking and enjoying this small break in the day, we both parted ways and returned to work.

"Hello, Lisa. It's a wonderful day today."

"That must have been some lunch, Ms. Washington."

"It was just what I needed, Lisa. Did I have any calls?"

"Nothing too important that I couldn't handle, but I'm still glad you're back."

I went back into my office to get through the rest of the workday. Every once in a while I would put my nose on my dress to smell it because it had remnants of his cologne from our goodbye embrace. It felt good to have a man's smell on me again, and a young, handsome one at that. Sleeping alone gets kind of old after a while, but I never saw myself being eye candy to a young man with his looks. But it feels good knowing I still got it. I got through the day and headed home. First thing I did was to run a nice hot bath tossing in some Bath and Body Works bubble bath while lighting a few candles to set the mood. When the tub was ready I went downstairs to get a glass of wine. I put my CD of love songs on before climbing into the tub, to make it all complete.

"Oh, yes. This is just what the doctor ordered," I said out loud.

A few sips later and I found myself totally relaxed, drifting off to dreamland. The thoughts running through my mind needed to be cast out by the laying on of hands. After about an hour, I blew out the candles and let the water out because this was starting to go somewhere it shouldn't ever go.

I was about to dry off when I heard the doorbell ring. Quickly, dropping the towel, I put on my bathrobe and headed downstairs. Now who in the world could this be at my door? It better not be Howard with his foolishness. When I opened the door I couldn't believe my eyes.

"Good evening, Ms. Washington. Hope I didn't catch you at a bad time."

"Well, I was just getting out of the bathtub. What are you doing here with these roses and that bottle of wine?"

"Being I'm a good listener, I heard you when you said your morning was eventful, so I wanted to make sure your evening ended better. Can I come inside or should I leave?"

"Of course. Please have a seat in the living room, I'll be right back."

"Wait, Sandra. You're fine the way you are. Come have a seat with me."

We walked into the living room taking a seat on the sofa. "Malachi, I'm not sure about this."

"Sandra, just trust me on this one. Lay back and allow me to give you a massage, alright? I promise I will keep my hands right where they belong."

Chapter 5

When I awoke the next morning I was upstairs in my bed. I looked under the cover and realized I was completely naked. I jumped up out of bed, and ran over to my bedroom door when I smelled the aroma of bacon.

"Oh, no. Lord, please tell me nothing happened last night with that man. Look at me asking the Lord about last night like I want to bring Him into this," I said rushing into the bathroom to jump in the shower.

I needed to go down and see what he was still doing in my house, but I just wanted to wash off whatever happened last night. I went into deep prayer, washing as fast as I possibly could to get every spot on my body.

"Lord, please forgive me for any and all sins that might have transpired in this house last night. Please bless this soap and water, and wash a sister clean, Lord. I don't want to present myself in anything less than acceptable in your sight. In Jesus' name, amen."

After drying off, I made my way downstairs to see what was going on in my kitchen.

"Well good morning, sunshine. How did you sleep?"

I just stood there dumbfounded watching him placing food on the table as if he had lived here for years. The expression on his face was giving off the vibe like something had happened between us.

"Malachi, why are you still in my house, and what are you doing in my kitchen?"

"Don't you remember anything that happened last night?"

"If I did would I be standing here asking you that question?"

"Have a seat and eat your breakfast before it gets cold and I will explain."

He sat my plate down on the table and pulled out my chair. When I took my seat he planted a soft kiss on my right cheek.

"Malachi, stop and tell me what happened last night. Please."

"Sandra, don't get your panties in a bunch when nothing happened that you didn't want to. You were in it as much as I was."

"In what, Malachi? I can't remember."

"Let's just say that I was totally surprised at the things you could do with your body. You were a straight freak."

"I don't believe I allowed myself to compromise my Christian faith by sleeping with you," I said breaking down in tears.

"Don't cry, baby girl; I made sure we did only what you wanted."

"Malachi! You took advantage of me while I was drunk, so don't try and spin the story to make yourself look so innocent. You date raped me and you know it. I should have you arrested."

"Hold on one second, Sandra! Don't pull that card on me when it was you that opened the door and allowed me into your home. When you saw me standing there with the roses and bottle of wine you already knew what it was, and the way you were dressed, or should I say not dressed sent a clear message of what you wanted. We both knew last night was coming."

"You're not concerned about how the Lord is feeling about what we did last night, or is it that you don't even care long as you got what you wanted?"

"I don't understand you women. You pray and cry to the Lord for a good man, and then when he sends Mr. Right into your life, look at how you act."

"Who said I was praying for a man, and what makes you think if I did it would be you?"

"Sandra, Sandra, Sandra, calm down, please. We both know how you were pushing up on me that Sunday in church. You got what you wanted and you know it."

"Just get out of my house right now, Malachi! I don't want you here any longer."

"I'll leave, but you will want me here later, so I'm not worried about that. Goodbye, Sandra."

I followed him to the front door. "I'm glad you are so sure of yourself," I said slamming the door in his face.

After locking it back, I just sat on the floor with my back to the door with both hands on my face as the tears began running down my face. He was right about what he said. I was praying for a husband. I need the Lord to send me a man who will love and treat me right. Howard did things to me that I don't care to bring up ever again. I tried for the last year to erase them from my mind and move on with my life. Everything was going just fine as long as I was not in the house. I don't care what people say, sleeping alone is so underrated. I woke up one night around 3:00a.m. in a cold sweat from a nightmare I had about dying alone. I jumped up out of bed, got down on my knees, and prayed to the Lord to send me a man. From that night on, every time I was in the church, I would pray hard for this to happen. That Sunday when I saw Malachi come sit next to me, I just knew he was sent from God. He was a little younger than

I would have expected, but I wasn't about to question the Lord's decision. I didn't want to rush into anything too soon, but when he showed up in front of my house I knew that it was divine intervention. They say a man who finds a wife, finds a good thing. Since he found me it had to be heaven-sent. Malachi was also right about seeing him again too. Now that I gave myself to him in the bedroom we are tied together whether I like it or not. Our spirits have crossed paths and our souls are connected now.

Well, I can't sit here on this floor forever. I got up going back into the kitchen to clean everything up before getting ready for work. When that was done, I went up to take a shower. Coming out the shower while drying off I was thinking to myself that I was glad it was Wednesday because of Bible study. This would give me a chance to talk with Pastor Blake. Last thing I did before leaving was strip the bed down and toss everything into a trash bag. I know I'm not a virgin, but I should have waited until marriage before jumping into bed with a man.

One night stands don't always led to a wedding ring. I went out to my car, popped open the trunk, and tossed the trash bag inside. I knew I couldn't blame it on the wine because I wasn't drunk when I let him come inside while I was wearing nothing but a bathrobe. I was old enough to know where it was headed which meant I could have stopped it. Sending mixed signals got my behind in this mess. I stopped by the fist dumpster I could find that was far enough from my house to get rid of the sheets. It wasn't going to solve anything I just didn't want them sex spirits laying up in my house all day. I drove up to the bank doing my usual look inside before pulling into the parking garage. Pulling my little bottle of anointing oil from the glovebox, I poured a little onto my hands rubbing it in as deep as I could get before getting out.

"Good morning, Ms. Washington. I see someone has that glow this morning."

"What glow is that, Lisa?"

"You know that he-put-it-on-me-last-night glow, girl."

"What you know about that glow, Lisa? And nobody put anything on me if you must know."

"I'm not saved and in church like you, so I get that glow put on me every chance I get. You can lie but the glow will tell on you every time."

I didn't even respond to her last statement. I just went into my office closing the door behind me. Walking over and taking a seat, all I could do was sit there with the look of embarrassment all over my face. I didn't realize Lisa had been watching my walk with Christ. The example I must be setting in her eyes right now can't be good, and I been trying to get her to come to church with me for some time now. My outward appearance is the light that people judge my walk with the Lord with. The Bible says in Matthew 5:16: *Let your light so shine before men, that they may see your good works, and glorify your Father which is in heaven.*

"I need to fix this right now," I said pulling my cell phone from my purse.

"Well, I guess I was right about you coming to me."

"Shut up, Malachi. I didn't call to hear you gloat about your conquest. We need to talk for real about what took place last night."

"I'm all ears, sweetheart. What's on your mind?"

"Not over the phone, I want to have this conversation in person. I'll get off early and we can meet at Piedmont Park. We can have a nice walk together while we talk things over, alright?"

"I might have other plans this afternoon, but let me check my schedule first."

"Don't play that game with me, Malachi. I'm not someone you want to see get upset."

"If it's anything like last night I might just take my chances," he said laughing.

"Are you meeting me or what!?"

"Don't blow a gasket, Sandra. I'll be there."

"You are so full of yourself. See you at noon."

"I can't wait to see you also," he said with a sarcastic tone before hanging up the phone.

Slamming the phone on the desk, I tried my best not to let his last statement take me to a bad place. Lord knows I need to be clearer in my prayer requests from now on.

"Ms. Washington, there is a Pastor Blake here to see you."

"Lord, I know you reveal everything but did you have to bring my mess to the light this quick?" I said to myself getting up from my desk.

I didn't have to walk out to the lobby because he was coming into the office already. "Pastor, what brings you downtown this morning?"

"Sister Washington, can I have a few minutes of your time? You were in my spirit this morning during my prayer time. Is everything alright?"

"Please, come in and have a seat. I was going to speak with you after Bible study tonight, but I guess now is a good time."

"Sister Washington, you look stressed about whatever it is that is on your mind."

"Pastor Blake, the last few days for me have been more then I'm used to dealing with. I'm thinking about starting a new relationship with a gentleman I met, and I want to get your input before I move forward."

"First, I'm glad that is all it is because I was truly worried for your wellbeing. If this is something you feel you are ready and able to handle after the divorce then you deserve to be happy. But, you already know my thoughts on premarital relations between a man and a woman."

"After 100 or more Sunday sermons, Pastor Blake, everyone knows how you and the Lord feel on that subject," I said laughing.

"Then what is your biggest concern about this new man whom I hope to meet soon?"

"Let's just say I may have a few years on him in age, and I don't want people judging me."

"People are going to judge you until the day you die, and if you are following the Word of the Lord your whole life will be viewed under a microscope. Long as you make sure whatever you do lines up with the Word, don't worry about the naysayers."

"I will, Pastor Blake. That is a promise."

"Glad to hear that. Now, let me get out of your office so you can get back to work. Hope to see you tonight at Bible study."

"I wouldn't miss it for anything in the world. Thank you, Pastor, for coming down to see me this morning."

I walked him to the door where we shared a hug before getting back to work. I didn't go into much detail about Malachi because I wasn't sure how to label our relationship just yet. I sure wasn't about to confess we had been intimate already. That would have given that old man a heart attack in my office. Plus, I sure couldn't show my face back in the Faith of Abundance Church of God no time soon. Let me just do these five loan applications so I can get out of here for today. I'm feeling good, so all are approved.

Chapter 6

"Alright, Lisa, I'm heading out for today so send all my calls to voicemail, please."

"Have a good afternoon, Ms. Washington."

After letting Mr. Jones know I was leaving for the rest of the day, I drove over to the park to meet up with Malachi.

"Where are you? I'm in the parking lot now."

"I'll be there in about five minutes, alright?"

"I told you what time I was going to be here so you wouldn't keep me waiting. I knew you would start acting like this."

"Acting like what, Sandra?"

"Don't act stupid, Malachi. You know how you guys act after getting what you want."

"Slow your roll, Sandra. There was a big accident so I had to wait until they cleared the cars out of the way. Your mind is running wild today."

"I'm so sorry for saying that, so please forgive me. I hope no one was hurt."

"They took one person to the hospital. Are you sure you're up for a walk in the park today? I don't need any negative energy around me."

"I told you I was sorry already. It will be fine just get here when you can. Goodbye."

I sat in the car for another half hour till he pulled up next to me. I rolled down the window trying my best not to go off on him.

"That traffic was something else. You ready to take that nice walk in the park?"

"Ready as I'm going to get, sweetheart," I said getting out of the car smiling."

"Don't you look fantastic in your red outfit," he replied walking around placing a soft kiss on my cheek.

"Get your lips off me and let's go before I change my mind."
"Alright, remember what I said about the negative vibe because there is other places I can be right now."

I didn't say another word because I was about to let him have it. I started walking towards the park entrance so we could talk about this so-called relationship. He caught up, taking my hand trying to ease the tension.

"I'm sorry, Sandra. I see this really means a lot to you."

I broke down crying at that point. "I still can't believe I slept with you."

"Get over it already and stop crying over spilled milk," he replied not even trying to comfort me.

"Malachi, you're an ass. I'm over here in tears and you're just standing over there doing nothing about it."

"I'm not trying to be insensitive, but we can't change what's been done. Let's go to dinner tonight and enjoy a nice evening together."

"I have Bible study tonight that I will not be missing."

"The Lord don't give his people time off to enjoy themselves?"

"His people? Don't you count yourself as one of his people, Malachi?"

"I never told you I was saved, Sandra."

"Then why did you come to Church?"

"I told you, I wanted to hear Pastor Blake speak. He's always bashing sin and sinners."

"Now, I feel like a fool for sure. You sure pulled the wool over my eyes with your fancy suits and smooth talking."

"Sandra, for the last time, you saw just what you wanted to see. You wanted a man so here I am. Just because I'm not saved means you can't even consider the possibility of me being the one your God sent into your life? By the look on your face I guess I've got my answer. All you Christians are so judgmental."

He turned around and started walking away. "Malachi, wait; don't leave. I'm not trying to judge you in any way. I've been through so much with my ex-husband that I don't want to repeat."

"Then come out with me tonight so I can show you how a real man treats a lady."

"What about Bible study?"

"I'm sure that you are not going to burn up if you miss one Bible study."

"You're right, and I want to spend time with you too. I took the rest of the day off so if you want to do something..."

"I would love to, Sandra, but I have a meeting I need to attend this afternoon."

We walked around for about another hour before heading back to the parking lot. I gave Sandra a kiss on the lips before getting into my car. I reached into the glovebox, and pulled out a napkin to wipe off any excess lipstick which might have come off during our exchange. I drove straight across town and went up to the 'meeting'. When I opened the door, she was already there laying on the bed in a black Victoria Secret's negligee. Her name is Keisha. 5'6, brown skin, brown eyes, slim build, wide hips, and legs for days. She has short black hair, but she is always wearing it in braids halfway down her back.

"It took you long enough, Malachi. So, how is my dear aunt doing today?"

"Keisha, are you sure about doing this to your own family?"

"Don't get soft on me now when things are going according to plan. You never had a problem before so what gives now? Don't tell me you are falling for that old woman."

"I'm good. What did she do so bad that you want to run this scam on her in the first place?"

"My dear sweet, Auntie Sandra always thought she was better than everyone else. She's always pushed that Bible down my throat like I was the worst thing on the planet. She always turned her nose up at me and my family just because I lived in the hood. I tried to go to her church a few times, but because of the way I was dressed they would turn me away. I couldn't help it if all I had to wear was tight little dresses. How was I supposed to change if they didn't let me see there was a different way to live my life? So, I went back to the streets, and three kids later I was forced to drop out of school. I had to do whatever I needed to do because they needed food on the table and clothes on their backs. So, here we are today. Why you trippin' anyways? You didn't have a problem with it that night I met you in the bar. You're getting paid and eating your cake on both sides at the same time."

"What's in this for you is my question?"

"I want you to pull her so far from her God that she will be begging for grace and mercy."

"You are one cold-blooded sister. I would hate to cross you. I'll continue going forward with your plan, and I'll do as you say for right now."

"Good. Now get over here and let me give you some motivation."

I spent a few hours in the room with Keisha before leaving. Sandra had been trying to call my cell. I played the voicemail to see what she wanted.

"Malachi, I was just calling to let you know I was thinking about you. Can't wait until tonight. Bye."

I pressed delete while laughing out loud. She's starting to lean a little more which is good. Just need to find that weakness to push her all the way over. Her spirit might be saved but her flesh still has weak points, and I just need to find them. I jumped on the bypass headed downtown when I realized there was no reason. I took the first exit and went back over to my apartment and started playing with my X-Box Live since I didn't have a real job to go to. I been doing this so long that I was starting to confuse myself about which lifestyle was real. After a few hours I fell asleep on the sofa. I was awakened by my cell phone ringing.

"Hey, Sandra. What's up?"

"It's after 7:30p.m. If you had told me you weren't coming I would have went to Bible study."

"I'm sorry about the time. I was in a late meeting, but I'm on my way right now."

"I can drive down to your house to save time if you tell me which one is yours because I know you may want to change clothes."

"Oh no. That won't be necessary. I'll just come pick you up. Then, we can pick up where we left off this afternoon. Plus, being seconds away from you makes me want you that much more."

"Since you put it that way I'll be right here waiting."

I tossed the phone on the sofa and rushed into the bedroom to change. Now, which one of these rented suits will I be wearing tonight? Running this game is expensive, but the rewards are worth every penny. Her funds will be my funds soon enough. I picked out the gray one and laid it across the bed while I jumped into the shower. After getting dressed and putting on a little Dolce & Gabbana, I headed out the door.

"What's up, Marcus? Still running game I see. When you going to stop playing with women?"

"Now Blue, I don't disrespect your street name so pay me the same respect, alright? When I'm dressed like this my name is Malachi which I done told you 100 times."

"We cool, bro. Who you got on the hook this time?"

"I'm freelancing my services out this time, but the mark is some older church woman who has the hots for some young meat. They might put on that show for the Pastor, but that flesh be calling them like that crack be calling you. I'm just cashing in on the beef one of her family members has with her."

"Alright, but you stay around them church folks long enough you're gonna catch that Jesus thing they be talking about. Speaking of crack let me hold a little something till I get paid."

"Fool, you don't have no job like me, and I'm not worried about that Jesus thing either. Look around this place. Does it look like God comes to the projects to you?"

"I might be a crackhead, but even I know He is everywhere. We choose our own fate by our actions and the way we treat other people."

"Take this 10 spot and get out my face before I..."

He ran off down the street before I could say anything else. I got into my car and watched him stumble and fall down a few times before he was out of sight. Blue was the neighborhood crackhead who was always begging for money to get his next fix. Always smelling like last year's trash with clothes on so old the name tags done wore off. I used to give him shoes but he kept selling them. He got his name from almost dying six times. He coded each time causing his lips to turn blue, but they always hit him with that juice to bring him back. Some say he was deep into church before he got strung out because he's always preaching about God. I just feel if the Lord was real then why would He allow Blue to run around the hood like this? Until I get that answer, I'll keep doing me. I headed out the complex watching out for all the kids running all over the place. I need to get over to Sandra's before she tries to find my house which doesn't exist. I wish I could afford to live in her area, but unless I hit the lottery that's not happening.

Chapter 7

I pulled up to her house just as she was walking out the front door. I made it just in time.

"I told you I was on my way, Sandra."

"That was over an hour ago, Malachi. I was just about to get in my car and ride around until I found your house. Why can't I see where you live?"

"Never said you couldn't come over. I was late because I was killing a large black snake that was outside the front door. There was another one that got away, but if you want to see my house let's go right now," he said walking around to open the passenger door.

"There is no way I'm going near that house with snakes crawling around. You need to call one of those exterminator companies to come out."

"Yes, I'll give them a call tomorrow to schedule a time. Then, you can come around anytime you feel like it, alright?"

"Let's just see about the snakes first. Well, its late now so what do you have planned?"

"How about we go over to Apache Café and have a few drinks?"

"Are you out of your mind? On a Bible study night!? I don't think so. Someone may see me in that place."

"Sandra, stop being so caught up in what other people think. You have the right to enjoy yourself like anyone else. Isn't it the Lord who gives musicians their talent in the first place? So why wouldn't He want you enjoying their gifts? I don't think you are going to burn up if you walk in the door."

"Are you trying to be sarcastic, Malachi?"

"Not at all. I'm just trying to get you to understand that jazz music will not send you to hell, that's all."

I stood there looking down at the ground just thinking of what hell would be like if the ground opened up and swallowed me right now. If I go and someone from church sees me then that would be bad, but if I don't go he may think I'm a stuck up Christian who thinks she's better then everyone. Well, I done slept with the man, so what else could happen?

"Let's go before I change my mind, and wipe that silly grin off your face. You're not slick."

We drove over to the club which was in the downtown area. I was looking around while trying to push my purse under my seat.

"This area doesn't look safe at all to me, Malachi."

"Sandra, nothing is going to happen to you while you're with me. Plus, I come here all the time so everyone knows me. How much safer can you get than that? Now, let me find a parking space then we can go inside."

We parked and started walking toward the entrance. I held his arm tight as I could to feel safe. I should have took my behind to church. Instead, I'm out here trying to keep some young man happy."

"Let up on your grip a little before you cut off my circulation," he said laughing.

When we walked inside I was overwhelmed with so much going on. We found a table and he ordered us a couple of drinks.

"This place isn't as bad as you thought it was, right? If any of your church friends are here then they thinking the same thing you are."

"It's not bad at all. It's just been so long since I've been to a place like this. Since my divorce my time is spent between work and church."

"Let's see if we can't loosen you up a little. Here, try this drink out," he said passing me a colored drink which looked like iced tea.

"What is this, Malachi? I don't drink hard liquor."

"Just give it a try before you poke your lips out. I'm not going to let anything happen to you. Don't you trust me, sweetheart?"

"Yes, I just don't want to get hurt or go against my Christian values."

"I got you, so drink up and enjoy yourself," he said taking me by the hand.

A few hours later, along with a few more drinks, I was feeling good about being out. The music was sounding good to my ears and having a good-looking man to stare at didn't hurt either. We stayed till around midnight before heading back home.

"I enjoyed myself so much tonight, and I have you to thank for that."

"You are so welcome. I'll get out of here so you can go to bed now."

"What about the snakes at your house?"

"I should be fine, and if not, at least I had a great evening with a beautiful woman."

"Just thinking about it is making my skin crawl. Please, come inside and spend the night."

"Sandra, are you sure about this because you remember what happened last time. I don't want you trippin' in the morning."

"That was a mistake, and it won't happen again. I'm concerned about your safety, and the way my head is still spinning I couldn't do anything if I wanted to. You can sleep in the guest bedroom, and I'll find you something to wear."

"Alright, only because I don't want you to worry, plus you look like you're about to pass out any second now."

We went into the house and I showed him where everything was like he didn't already know. We both pretended like it was his first time being upstairs.

"Well, I guess you have everything you need, so I'll see you in the morning."

"Goodnight, Sandra. Thank you again for trusting me enough to spend the night."

I watched her stumble down the hallway until she was in her room. Those two long island iced teas must have taken a toll on her. I was just about to change and get into bed when my cell phone started ringing.

"What's up, Keisha?"

"Don't what up me. I'm at your place looking for you and you're not here."

"I was coming after I dropped off your aunt, but she wouldn't let me leave."

"Where is that old bat now?"

"She is probably laying across the bed passed out. I had her drinking long island iced teas at Apache Café tonight."

"I can't believe you got her to go out on a church night. You are on your game that's for sure. I'll be over in about 10 minutes so meet me at the back door."

"I don't think that is a good idea right now, Keisha."

"Nobody is asking you, stupid. Don't forget I'm the brains and you are just the eye candy. If I want your input on anything I'll give it to you."

She hung up before I could say anything. Her coming over here can't be a good thing. I walked down to Sandra's room to see if she was sleeping, and just like I thought she was passed out across the bed. I went downstairs to wait for Keisha to show up. She pulled up into the driveway with her headlights turned off.

"Open the door and let me inside, stupid," she yelled while turning the doorknob.

"I told you she was knocked out across the bed so there is nothing we can get done tonight."

"Again you're talking when nobody asked for your opinion. I knew you wouldn't take advantage of this great opportunity so I'm here to fix things. Let's go upstairs and get you in place."

"Get me in place," I said to myself as we walked back up.

"Look at her high and mighty behind laying there drunk. If only her little church group could see her now. Help me get her into bed, stupid."

"What is your plan, Keisha?"

"Malachi, is that you? Is someone in here with us because it sounds like a female's voice?"

"It's just me, sweetheart. I'm trying to get you into bed before you fall on the floor," I said as Keisha ran back into the hallway.

"Must be the alcohol talking then. Help me get out of these clothes before I mess them up."

"Alright, sit up so we can get you undressed then into bed, so I can go back to my room."

By the time I had her shoes off she was passed out again. Keisha came running into the room.

"Hurry up and get your clothes off, and I'll get her undressed. I'm not going to miss this opportunity to bring her down to my level. All those times when she would talk down on my lifestyle and about me to her friends; look at her now."

"Wow. You really hate this woman don't you?"

"I hate what she stands for. She's always coming off like she never done anything wrong in her life, and people like us are beneath her. Now, get in bed beside her so I can snap these pictures."

"Wait! I never agreed to any pictures naked or with your aunt. You are taking this too far."

"I'll take this as far as I need to, and don't you forget who is running this show," she said slapping me upside the head.

I got into bed and positioned myself just as Keisha instructed. The look in her eyes as she snapped each picture was of pure evil.

"Move your body closer and pull that cover back some more and put your arm across her chest. Don't mess this up for me, Malachi."

"Just hurry up and take the pictures before she wakes up again. I'm not feeling this whatsoever."

"Alright, I got what I needed. Let's go back downstairs so I can tell you what the next move is going to be."

After putting my clothes back on, we went down into the kitchen. I was so disturbed by what just happened I fixed a strong drink to calm myself back down.

"What do you plan to do with those pictures?"

"Don't worry yourself about these pictures one bit. I just need you to start working on her money because I have bills that need paying."

"Remind me never to cross you because you're the devil's daughter in the flesh."

"Just you keep that thought in your head and things will be fine. I'm out of this place because I'm starting to itch from all the uppity stuff in this house."

I watched her back out of the driveway and take off. Just as I was putting my glass in the sink, I heard my name being called.

"Malachi! Who are you talking to down there? I heard a female's voice coming from my kitchen."

It was Sandra standing at the top of the stairs wearing nothing. I had to think of something quick.

"Hey, sweetheart. What are you doing out the bed? I just came down to get something to drink and was watching the television for a second. I must have had it up too loud. I'm so sorry for waking you."

"That voice sounded so familiar, but I can't put my finger on who that was."

"Sandra, why would I have someone in your home this late? Let's get you back to bed."

Chapter 8

The next morning when I woke up, Sandra was standing over my bed just watching me.

"How long have you been standing here?"

"Good morning, honey. I haven't been here long at all. I just wanted to thank you for being a perfect gentleman last night. I don't remember much from last night, but when I woke up alone in bed I felt good about whatever might have happened."

I just looked at her for a few minutes before responding because I didn't know if she was waiting to catch me in a lie.

"You were out of it last night after we got back, so I just put you in the bed. You do remember asking me to stay over, right?"

"Of course I do, silly. Now, come on downstairs so I can make us some breakfast before we head off to work."

"I'll be down right after I take a shower and get dressed, alright?"

"I'll have everything waiting for you."

She left and I went into the bathroom. This is working to perfection. Now, it's on to the money.

After getting dressed, I put on my clothes from last night before going downstairs.

"Everything smells delicious, Sandra."

"I didn't hear you come down. Please, have a seat and I'll make your plate."

"I was wondering if you have seen my wallet because I couldn't find it anywhere."

"Are you sure you didn't leave it in the car last night?"

"You might be right about that. Let me run out there and check right quick."

When I got to the car, I placed my wallet underneath the driver's seat and then acted like I was looking for it. After a few minutes I went back inside.

"I must have dropped it somewhere coming out the bar last night."

"All of your credit cards and personal information is out there somewhere. You need to call and cancel your cards before someone uses them."

"You're right," I said as I pulled out my cell phone to make a fake call to the bank.

"What did they say?" she asked, as I was hanging up.

"They were able to cancel the cards but someone had used one of them already this morning. She said it would be about a week before I can get replacement cards sent out."

"I sure hate that happened, and I kind of feel responsible in a way. Let me get my purse and give you something to hold you over until you get your new cards."

"Sandra, I can't let you do that. I'll be alright for a few weeks."

She didn't say a word as she walked out the kitchen, returning with her checkbook. She sat down at the table and started writing out a check.

"Here you go. I think this should hold you over until your replacement cards come in the mail," she said handing me the check.

"Sandra, this is a check for $1,500. Are you sure about this?"

"Look, if I can't trust someone who lives down the street from me then who can I trust. Take this check and don't worry about it."

"I don't know how to thank you for such generosity. This should get me through just fine."

"Well, it's time I go up and get ready for work. You can let yourself out when you are done eating."

When I was done eating breakfast I left and drove over to the bank to cash the check before heading back over to my apartment to change clothes and play a few games on the X-Box. Walking through the door, I tossed the cash on the coffee table then went into the kitchen to get a cold beer from the refrigerator. When I turned around I dropped the can in shock.

"What are you doing here, Keisha?"

"I see you got some money out of Auntie dear, but this is just the start of things to come. I'll just take half so can I get my hair and nails done."

"I knew giving you a key was a major mistake. What do you want now?"

"I wanted to know how things went before I go to the salon to get my Brazilian hair redone."

"You see the money in your hand so you know how things went."

"Don't let spending time over in that uppity neighborhood catch you a beat down. You already know not to come at me like that. Sit down and let me go over what I need you to do next."

"I'll be glad when this is over, so you and I can part ways."

"What would you do without me watching out for you?"

"I'd get a job and take care of myself like I been doing, and I can always get another female."

"Right, like you can give all this up. We both know you're not getting a real job in this lifetime, so shut up and listen carefully."

I knew she was right about the job thing, so I walked over taking a seat beside her to hear what her next move was going to be. The more she laid out her master plan I couldn't help but to feel sorry for Sandra being caught up in her rage. She stayed a few more hours before leaving. I was so tired by then I fell asleep on the sofa.

I got to work a little late this morning because I tried to find Malachi's house to give him a kiss. I must have ridden through five times without seeing his car which left me a little uneasy, but I didn't get too bent out of shape when I remembered him telling me about the snakes. He must have taken his clothes to work to get dressed so he wouldn't get bitten. I'll just get him to tell me which one it is so I can stop by after work this afternoon. I parked then walked inside.

"Good morning, Ms. Washington. I see someone has herself a new man."

"Good morning, Lisa. How you come to that conclusion?"

"First, the way you're walking in here late which you never do, and second, you got your skirt on backwards," she said laughing.

I looked down to see what she was talking about. Not saying another word, I walked into my office locking the door so I could turn it around. Of course I couldn't do nothing but laugh at myself. As I unlocked the door and went over to my desk a big smile came over my face.

It felt good having a man back in my life even if he is 20 years younger. I feel like a school girl again. My cell phone started ringing just as I was about to get started working. It was coming from a blocked number.

"Hello? Who is this, please?"

"Don't you recognize my voice, Auntie?"

"What do you want, Keisha? I told you last year after you came to my job and showed your behind we were done."

"Auntie, are you still salty about something that happened last year? What that Bible of yours tell you about holding on to animosity towards your fellow man?"

"Look, you little ghetto child from hell. I don't have time for your nonsense this morning."

"There you go. I knew you had some hood buried in them old bones of yours somewhere. I just called to see if you would let me hold a little something."

"You called me at my job to ask a stupid question. It will be a cold day in hell before you see one dime of my money ever again, and do yourself and me a favor by losing this number!"

"It must be a little chilly in hell today then, and I just sent you a picture of my new Brazilian hair. Bye, Felicia. You have a blessed day."

"Wait!" I said but she hung up on me.

That child is a piece of work. I see why my sister wanted her to move out here before they killed each other. I didn't take her statement seriously because sarcastic comments are always coming out her dirty mouth. I deleted the picture without even looking at it and went back to what I was doing. Keeping her away from Malachi will be my top priority. The last thing I need is for her to mess this up for me by trying to seduce him with her fast behind. Speaking of Malachi, that's him calling now...

"Hello, Malachi. I was just thinking about you."

"I hope it was something good. I was just calling to let you know I won't be able to return to my house for a few days while the exterminators deal with the snakes. Apparently, there were more than I anticipated them finding."

"I hate to hear that. Where will you stay?"

"Don't worry about me because I already booked a room at a hotel."

"I can't let you spend your money on a room when I have all that space at my home. You said it's only for a few days, so why don't you pack what you need, and come stay with me."

"Sandra, I can't impose on you like that."

"I will not take no for an answer. There is a spare key located in a security box on the left side of the front door and the code is 316. Make yourself at home, and I'll see you later tonight after I attend this meeting for the company."

"I would like to stay close where I can keep an eye on things at my house. I don't know how to thank you for this, Sandra."

"I'm sure you will think of something, Malachi. I need to run now so talk to your later. Bye."

I hung up the phone with a big smile on my face. Guess the Lord worked things out without my help. This way I don't have to worry about Keisha coming over. My day just got a whole lot better after that conversation. Now back to work.

I just laughed as I was putting my cell phone back into my pocket. Sandra is more stupid than I thought if she fell for that story. Well, being I don't have a real job and she is going to be home late tonight, why don't I just head over to her house now. Let me just pack a few of these good suits along with a bag to keep up the façade. That reminds me, I need to go pay on this rental car. She is going to try and get me to go to that church with her since I'm staying there, so a nice plan is in order. I'll get one of my boys to call me on Sundays with an urgent personal matter that needs to be taken care of. Being in church always makes me feel uneasy with all that singing and preaching. I love me some church women because they are so loyal when you get into that mind and heart. I headed out the front door and ran straight into Blue.

"Why are you always around my door, Blue?"

"You the only one that don't be trippin' on me around here. Where you off to?"

"Watch my spot for a few days while I take care of some church business."

"I might be a crackhead, but I know not to play with the Lord's people."

"Just do it, Blue," I said driving off.

After getting over to Sandra's house, first thing I did was start looking for anything with personal information on it. I need to open a few accounts so I can do some shopping. She has all these church programs all over the place. I don't understand why they keep them so long when that service is not going to happen again. What is this beat up old thing in this drawer? I pulled it out and wiped the dust off so I could read what it said. It's a plaque with something from the book of Matthew 7:15-20. It reads: **Beware of false prophets, which come to you in sheep's clothing, but inwardly they are ravening wolves. Ye shall know them by their fruits. Do men gather grapes of thorns, or figs of thistles? Even so every good tree bringeth forth good fruit; but a corrupt tree bringeth forth evil fruit. A good tree cannot bring forth evil fruit, neither can a corrupt tree bring forth good fruit. Every tree that**

bringeth not forth good fruit is hewn down, and cast into the fire. Wherefore by their fruits ye shall know them. Too late God, I'm already in the house and she belongs to me now.

Chapter 9

I couldn't wait to get out of the meeting and head home since I knew Malachi was there waiting on me. As soon as I pulled up into the driveway and saw his car, it put a big smile on my face. I was in such a rush to get inside that I almost dropped my briefcase on the ground. I laughed out loud and shook my head at myself. I took a moment to gather myself before going inside, so he wouldn't know how excited and eager I was to see him. When I walked in, the smell coming from the kitchen took my breath away.

"What is that smell?" I said walking into the kitchen.

"Well, good evening my dear. I knew you would be hungry after a long day, so I fixed you a little something."

"You call this a little something? Shrimp cocktail, prime rib, red potatoes, baked macaroni and cheese, and a garden salad."

"For dessert, I took the liberty of making you a chocolate mousse cake. I hope everything is to your liking. Please, have a seat and enjoy your meal while I go run you a bubble bath."

"You are truly a breath of fresh air that the Lord has sent into my life. If I'm dreaming please don't wake me up."

"Nothing you see before you is a dream, I assure you. I'll be back when everything is ready," he said while placing a soft kiss on my neck.

I held my composure together until I was halfway up the stairs. Just watching her eat up all the bull I was dishing out was priceless. I need an Emmy award for my performance on this scam. Going into the bathroom, I started the tub while pouring in some Bath and Body Works bubble bath. Reaching for one of the red roses I picked up on the way over, I pulled off the petals and dropped them into the water. Now I'm going to light these candles for the final mood setter, then I'll bring her up. "For a guy who plays video games all day this don't look half bad," I said to myself.

"Wow. Is this all for me?"

"Sandra, I didn't hear you come upstairs."

"I was starting to miss you down there. How can I ever repay you for all this kindness?"

"Why don't we drive down to Myrtle Beach and spend the weekend? I have a friend who owns a beach house there."

"Malachi, that is so tempting, but I can't miss church this Sunday because of missing Bible study already."

"Hard as you have been working and dealing with all the stress of the last few weeks don't you think you need to take a mini-vacation? I can't think of a better way than laying on the beach. I'm sure the Lord won't hold missing two services against you. We could have more intimate moments like this one but near the water."

"I would like to spend some alone time with you at the beach, but I just don't know."

"Let's get you into this bath before your water gets cold then we can continue this conversation."

I went into the room and took off my clothes then eased down into the water which felt so good. Looking into his eyes, I could tell he really wanted me to say yes to his request. In a way, my body was already saying yes on its own.

"Malachi, we can take that trip this weekend because I do need a change of scenery."

"Great. I'll take care of all the planning, and all you have to do is pack."

The smile that came over his face when I said yes was priceless. Keeping him happy is all I want to do right now. My prayers for a good man have been answered that is for sure.

"I'll leave you alone to enjoy your bath while I go down and clean up the kitchen."

"Alright, dear. I'll see you in a little while," I said giving him a soft kiss on the lips.

Again I started laughing going back down the stairs because of how easy it was talking her out of going to church. "See, I told you she belongs to me now, and there is nothing you can do about it," I said pointing up towards the celling. Well, let me go in here and clean this mess up.

"What the hell are you doing here!?"

"Keep your voice down, stupid. Where is my sweet auntie?"

"She's upstairs in the bathtub while I clean up the kitchen. How did you know I was here?"

"You know that crackhead Blue can't hold water which is a good thing because I see you over here playing house."

"You told me to break her, so that is what I'm doing. Why are you here, Keisha?"

"Look at you coming at me like a boss. Don't you let spending time up in here go to your head. It won't be good for your health. Now, what is your plan?"

"I talked her into spending time with me at the beach. She thinks we are going to stay at a friend's beach house, but we are staying at one of them timeshare things. I'll smooth it over when we get down there."

"You can do a little thinking on your own. I can't believe you talked her into missing church."

"She's right where I want her, and soon, I'll have everything she owns in my name. You need to get out of here before she hears your voice."

"I'm out, but don't try pulling a fast one or they will be reading your obituary at that church, understand?" she said while walking out.

I don't know how much more I can take of her pushing me around before I lose it. Right now I need to stay focused on the bigger objective which is Sandra. Speaking of her let me go up and see how things are going. I walked into the bathroom and started massaging her shoulders.

"Hello, pretty lady. How are you feeling?"

"I'm feeling good now that you're back. I was having the strangest dream before you walked in."

"I hope it was something good about me."

"You were in the dream, but it wasn't good. It was more like a nightmare because it involved my niece, Keisha, who I don't get along with at all. You and she were standing over my grave just laughing and kissing. Please tell me you don't know anyone by that name, and you would never do anything to hurt me?"

"Sandra, sweetheart, I would never do anything to hurt you in any way. Whatever happened in that dream could never come true as long as I'm here," I said holding her hands.

"I pray that's true, but you never denied knowing her," she said looking into my eyes.

"Of course I don't know any female with that name," I replied while staring back into her eyes just as deep.

I knew this was that moment my game had to be better than it's ever been or this scam was toast. I could feel her searching for the truth with each passing second that went by. My hands started heating up as she was holding them tight. This faith of hers might be trying to blow my cover wide open which can't happen right now.

"Look, let's not spoil the mood with a dream that's never coming true. After you get dried off, how about I give you a full body massage so you can relax?"

When I said that, her demeanor changed quickly to a big smile.

"Alright, but you remember what happened last time you gave me one," she said stepping out of the tub.

I followed her into the bedroom to get everything ready so I could get my plans back on track. She stretched out on the bed and I took over from there which turned intimate quickly.

I woke up the next morning before her and went into the guest room to start packing. The way things went last night in the bathroom made me realize we need to go down to the beach a day earlier.

"Good morning, honey. Why are you packing your bags, is your house ready?"

"No, it's not. I was thinking we should go down to the beach today and take advantage of all the time alone that we can get. I'll call and rent a hotel room while you pack."

"Wow. First, you put it on me last night, and now we're about to head to the beach. I was just getting ready to call in absent to work today, so we could spend the day together. Guess we both were thinking the same thing. Wait. I thought you said we were staying at a beach house."

"About that, my friend called me and said he had his dates mixed up and will not be able to give me the house this weekend. Don't worry because I made other plans already."

"You must have been up a few hours to get all that done before I woke up."

"Yes, now, go get packed so we can leave."

"You said that with a little bass in your voice. Is everything alright, Malachi?"

"Yes, I'm sorry for snapping at you. I just wanted this weekend to be special."

"Alright, I've just never seen this side of you that's all. I'll go get packed right now and meet you downstairs."

I went back into my room closing the door behind me. Before packing, I walked over and picked up my Bible to pray. Getting down on my knees I began to pray:

"Lord, I need to know if this is the man you have sent into my life. I pray and ask your forgiveness for being weak and sleeping with him in sin. Father, there is no excuse for my actions except lust of the flesh. Please send me a sign or something so I know if this relationship is healthy for me. In Jesus' name, amen."

Once I was done praying I packed everything I needed, and I went down to meet Malachi who was sitting in the living room waiting. But something about him seemed different. I tried giving him a kiss on the cheek, but he just got up and walked towards the front door without looking at me. Getting my bags which he could have carried out to the car, I didn't say anything until we were in the car.

"Thank you for putting my bags in the car, sweetheart."

"Sandra, are you trying to be sarcastic or just funny?"

"Wow. Look who done a 360-degree turn since we shared the same bed. Maybe this trip isn't necessary after all. Your true colors are starting to show now."

"I told you I was upset about having to go down earlier then we planned that's all. Stop reading into something that isn't there, please; if you want to cancel just open your door and get out."

"I said I would go so let's get on our way and please change your attitude before we get there," I said pulling out my cell phone.

"I hope that's not another man you're texting."

"Why are you trippin'? No it's not. I'm just playing a game. See?" I said sitting back wondering if this is the sign I prayed to the Lord for.

Chapter 10

Six months have passed since our little getaway to the beach, most of which we spent in the room. Malachi has completely moved into my house due to him having to sell his because of the snake problem. I never did get to see the inside of it or the location. Things between us have not been the same since before we slept together, but I wasn't going to give up on him just yet. I started missing more church services because he had me in the clubs and at late night bars. My coworkers even noticed how I was dressing differently these days. Malachi said I needed to change my style to match his. Short dresses and tight shirts were never my thing, but when you're dating someone younger than you keeping up is a must. Speaking of keeping up, that's him calling me now.

"Hey, sweetheart, are we still meeting for dinner tonight?"

"No, I'll be home late again because of these reports I need to get completed."

"Malachi, I haven't spent time with you in over a week now. What about my feelings?"

"I can always quit my job and stay home and your little feelings can pay all the bills. How does that sound, honey?"

"You can be an ass sometimes, Malachi. I guess I'll see you whenever you come home."

"Keep it hot for daddy, sweetheart. Bye now," he said before hanging up the phone.

I would go over to his job to give him a piece of mind if I wasn't tied up with these loan applications. Come to think of it, I have never been to his job. Well, since he's coming home late I'll go to Bible study tonight. I'm sure to get some strange looks when I walk in though.

Getting through the rest of the workday, I headed home to get something to eat before going to church. After I sat down at the kitchen table, I couldn't take one bite of the sandwich I fixed. I was still upset about my conversation with Malachi, so I ended up just tossing it into the trash can. Then I picked up my Bible and headed to the car. When I pulled into the church parking lot I noticed Sister Dean's car which meant there was going to be drama. "Lord, take the wheel and help me to hold my tongue," I said out loud as I was getting out the car.

"So you are just going to walk right past me without speaking?" a voice called out when I stepped into the lobby.

"Hello, Sister Dean. It's so good to see you."

"I would say the same thing, but I barely recognized who you were in that hoochie outfit you're wearing."

"Look, I just came to hear the Word if you don't mind, so keep your comments to yourself."

"Aren't we a little touchy tonight? You sure do need some Word to get rid of whatever evil spirits done pulled you out of church and got you dressing like a street walker. I'll pray for you, Sister Washington."

"Only thing you better pray for is that I don't come over there and put my foot in your behind. Now get out my face."

"You see, Sister Jones. This is what you become when you step out the will of the Lord. Let's go inside and pray for that sister."

I was so upset by the time I got into the main sanctuary, but Pastor Blake had already started the service. I took a seat towards the back so everyone wouldn't be focused on me. It felt funny sitting here after sleeping with Malachi, but I guess sinning will do that. Even now I'm trying my best to pull this little dress down but it keeps riding back up my hips. Shoot. I forgot to bring my Bible with me. Whenever Pastor Blake looked in my direction, I looked down as if I was reading something. It didn't work because he was now coming this way. He placed his hand on my shoulder while looking down into my eyes.

"Church, like we were talking about Sunday in the book of Proverbs 18:22: ***Whoso findeth a wife findeth a good thing, and obtaineth favor of the Lord.*** The Lord teaches you as a woman, to have patience and wisdom while you wait for Mr. Right, and not to settle for Mr. Right

Now. When you allow yourself to be pulled out of the will of the Lord to satisfy the desires of the flesh, everything becomes unblessed. Yes, you are riding high on emotions that this is going to last forever and nothing could ever break you apart. But, remember what it says in the book of Mark 10:9: ***What therefore God hath joined together, let not man put asunder.*** If the Lord is not in the midst of your relationship there will be nothing but problems when hard times come, and they will come. The flesh can only satisfy itself and will do anything to quench its thirst. That is why you must stay prayed up, and don't rob yourself of the fellowship of being in the house of the Lord. I know this message is meant for someone here tonight, and I pray you don't let it go into one ear and out the other. It's late so everyone let's bow our heads in prayer."

As I was sitting with my head down something told me he already knew about my relationship with Malachi. If he didn't, then this little dress done gave me away. The best thing for me to do is get up and make my way out to my car fast as possible. Just as I was getting my purse to leave he closed the prayer and everyone got up out their seats.

"Sister Washington, can I see you in my office before you leave, please?"

"Pastor Blake, I need to be getting home. Can this wait until another time?"

"I would say yes, but I'm not sure when and if you will come back to church. Let's head to my office."

He led the way into his office taking a seat at his desk. I took a seat in one of the leather wingback chairs while frantically trying to keep my dress down.

"Here you go, Sister Washington. Put this over your lap so we both are not uncomfortable. I keep a few prayer cloths in my office for when I have to counsel women."

"Thank you. Why did you want to see me?"

"I'm not going to beat around the bush here because we both can see by the way you're dressed that there is something going on in your life. You stopped coming to church, and you've been taking time off your job for days at a time. All this leads me to think that there is a man caught up in this somehow. Look at yourself sitting there dressed like you're about to walk the streets or dance at a one of them gentleman's clubs. What is going on with you, Sister Washington?"

His words hit me like a double-edged sword cutting right down to the bone. I could feel my tear ducts filling up, as I tried to find a tissue in my purse.

"Pastor, everything is fine. I'm just making a few changes in my life that people might not understand. If there is nothing else, I'll be leaving."

"I'm not going to pressure you to talk to me, but my door is always open. I'll walk you out to your car."

"That's alright, Pastor Blake, because I'm sure a few members stayed over to see what happened so they can have something to gossip about."

I got up holding the prayer cloth until I made sure my dress was pulled down then tried to hand it back to him.

"You can just place it in that basket by the door on your way out because you know how I feel about the transferring of spirits. Have a blessed evening, Sister Washington."

Not saying a word, I tossed it into the metal basket then walked out of his office. The way he looked at me sent shame through my whole spirit. When I got to the lobby, Sister Dean and another sister were standing off to the side looking in my direction. I wasn't about to leave without giving her a piece of my mind.

"I hope you both are getting your little laugh on at my expense."

"No one cares about your affairs or your life other than making sure you don't bring drama to this church."

"Only drama I'm going to bring is snatching that cheap weave out of your head and dragging you out in the parking lot to beat that behind. Now, get out the way so I can go home."

"Well, I guess somebody done lost their way."

I was so upset when I got into the parking lot that I didn't realize I was trying to unlock the wrong car with my remote. Getting inside I started beating my hand on the steering wheel. Getting myself together I made my way home so I could spend some alone time with Malachi. When I pulled into the driveway there was another vehicle that I didn't recognize. I just sat there for a few minutes feeling uneasy, like someone strange was in my home. Walking up to the front door there was loud talking and some type of loud noise. Opening the front door I was in complete shock at what I saw in the living room.

"Hey, sweetheart, I hope you don't mind that Kevin stopped by to play a few hours on the X-Box Live with me."

I just stood there with my mouth open while trying to let it all sink into my head because this fool clearly done lost his mind. He had hooked up some video game system to my 70-inch television, and also had beer cans all over my coffee and end tables. The volume was so loud that I could barely hear him talking. This Kevin dude was just sitting there with a stupid grin on his face.

"Malachi, I can't believe you are sitting in my living room playing video games with someone in my house who I don't even know, and let's not leave out this mess of beer cans all over my expensive tables."

"Calm down, baby girl. It's not that serious. Remember, this is our house now, and my friends are your friends now. You run along upstairs and I'll be up in a few hours, alright?"

"You are not going to stand there and send me up to my room like I'm some little child. Who do you think you are?"

"I'm the man you prayed for, remember? Don't forget that. Again, lower your voice and run along upstairs."

When I realized what he just said to me, I felt my chest start to tighten up and my eyes started to tear up.

"Don't start with the crying thing in front of company because it's not a good first impression."

"If I didn't just come from church I would tell you what I think of your behind right now."

"I wasn't listening. Did you say something?"

Fearing what I would do next I just went up to my room. Before I did anything I would regret later, I called one of my friends to vent to.

"Hey, Sandra. I was just about to call you, girl. I just got off the phone with Sister Jones who told me about the altercation between you and Sister Dean."

"Candice, I can't believe how church folks love to gossip and call themselves saved."

"Sandra, being saved don't have anything to do with loving to run your mouth. Women love to keep drama going and you know this. Now, why does it sound like you been crying?"

"It's Malachi. I came home to find him and some dude in my living room playing video games like two kids. Then, he disrespected me by trying to send me up to my room. Candice, I almost lost it."

"I would say I'm sorry to hear that, but moving a man you are not married to or even really know into your home is not the brightest thing in the world to do. You can keep trying to convince me that you haven't slept with him, but his young behind put it down and broke you."

"Alright, alright, so we slept together, but that doesn't give him the right to treat me like this."

"For someone who has a Master's and a PhD you are not bright in the relationship department. Sandra, haven't you ever heard of the phrase, "Why buy the cow when you can get the milk for free?"

"Yes, what does that have to do with me?"

"I'm sitting here shaking my head if you want to know. Being you done let him taste the goods without putting in any investment of himself, his respect for you is low. You need to be more careful what you pray for in the future. The Lord is never going to send you the perfect man because there is not one. He will, on the other hand, open the door allowing someone to come into your life to see if they match what your spirit needs. If your spirit is calling for lust, you can't blame God for what is happening."

"Candice, I called you to vent and not for you to be judgmental. I'm going to bed. Goodbye."

"Just keeping to real that's all. Bye."

Chapter 11

When I woke up the next morning, Malachi was not in the bed. I don't have time for this, is what I was thinking as I got up. Hearing noises coming from downstairs I went to see what it was.

"You have got to be kidding me! Please don't tell me you been down here all night playing that stupid game with this stranger in my house."

"Wow. I didn't realize how late it was. Guess we got carried away a little, but give me a few and I'll wrap this up."

"I'll tell you what, I'm going back upstairs to get ready for work, and you and your boy better not be here when I come back down."

"Kevin, you better get ready to leave so she don't embarrass herself no more than she is right now."

"I'll check you later, dude. I'm so glad my chick don't be trippin' like this."

I showed Kevin out before going into the kitchen to get a cup of coffee. Bringing the game over here may not have been a bright idea, went through my mind as I was starting up the Keurig.

"I hope you don't think I'm helping you clean up that mess in the living room."

"How in the world do you keep getting into this house, Keisha? You scared the life out of me."

"If I tell you then I'll have to kill you. Now, where is my sweet auntie?"

"She's upstairs getting ready for work and should be down anytime so you better get out of here."

"Don't worry about me. I need you to go up and slip one of her bank cards out her purse for me, so I can do a little shopping."

"You must be out your mind if you think I'm doing that."

"In that case, I'll just run up there and tell her all about our scam and how you were the mastermind of the whole thing. Let's see how long it takes for her to call the police and you to go to jail," she said walking towards the door.

"Wait! I'll go get it, but you better leave after that."

"Good. Run along and fetch my money, boy,"

"I hate everything you stand for, Keisha."

"You might want to take a long look in the mirror, slick. Don't worry I'll swing back through and tighten you up later today, sugar."

I went up to check where Sandra was before going for the card. She was still in the bathroom so I went over to the dresser to get her purse. Before I could get my hand back out she walked in on me.

"What are you doing in my purse, Malachi?"

"I wasn't in your purse. I was just getting this bandage for the cut on my finger."

"Let me see it because you may need stitches," she said walking over to me.

I put my finger in my mouth so she couldn't see it wasn't cut then walked out the room quickly.

"Here take this card and get out before she comes down."

"Thank you, sweetie," she said pulling it from my hand while placing a kiss on my cheek.

I went to see how she got in when I heard Sandra coming. I quickly put the Band-Aid on.

"So, you plan on going to work today or are you playing video games all day with your little friends?"

"I see you got jokes this morning. I'm on my way to take a shower right now if you want to know. Have a blessed day, honey."

"Don't forget to clean that mess up before you leave, and don't let this happen again."

"I'll see what I can do about that. Well, I don't want to be late," I said going out the kitchen.

Watching out the bedroom window, I waited until she pulled out the driveway then went back to the living room. Pushing the empty beer cans on to the floor, I placed a six-pack on the table before cutting the game back on.

"Alright! Who's online with me?"

"Malachi, what you doing back online already? I thought your old lady was home."

"What up, Kevin. She just left to go to work so I'm good. You want to come back over and play?"

"Man, I'm not with that drama you got going on at your place. How long you going to play her?"

"Bro, long as I can get away with it. This one is too easy. Can you believe her own niece hooked me up with this scam?"

"You need to be careful of Keisha on the real because she is only out for self. One more thing, bro, I don't go to church, but I know better than playing with church folks. I saw all the Bible stuff in her living room."

"Stop trippin', Kevin. That Bible mumbo jumbo only works if you believe in it."

"You better stop trippin' because you know there is a God. This has to be the lowest thing you done that I know of, and if you don't stop then you going to get a one-way ticket to hell."

"Dude, you sound like that crackhead Blue now. I can't believe we're talking about this online."

"We can't either, you going to hell. Now get offline," a voice yelled out.

"Kevin, I'll get with you later. I'm going to play for a few hours then take a nap before putting this place back together."

"Alright, remember what I told you about Keisha. She doesn't play good with others."

When I pulled into the parking garage at work, I sat in my car for a few minutes trying to gather myself before going inside. Looking into the rearview mirror, I'm starting to feel like a fool for getting involved with Malachi. Let me get out of this car before I ruin my makeup by crying. Walking down the sidewalk, men were staring at me and trying to get my attention which has never happened until I started wearing these little dresses. Even walking into the bank the stares didn't stop.

"Good morning, Ms. Washington. I almost didn't recognize you."

"Nancy, please come into my office. Close the door and have a seat, please."

"Is everything alright, Ms. Washington?"

"Nancy, you are about 23 or 24, correct?"

"I'm 23. Why are you asking?"

"Nancy, take a look at this dress and tell me if you would wear it," I said turning around.

"To be perfectly honest with you, I would only wear that to the club to get attention for men to buy me drinks all night."

"I must look like a fool to you because of me being a Christian."

"Ms. Washington, I don't go to church, but if I was thinking about going this is not a good look to base that decision on. I'm not just talking about this outfit, but also the way you have let your faith be compromised for the affections of a man. Wasn't the Lord strong enough to keep you and allow you to wait on the right person because of that whole 'I can do badly all by myself' thing?"

"This conversation has truly opened my eyes to how my lifestyle plays a big part of my walk with the Lord. Thank you, Nancy."

"Well, let me get out of here and go do my job."

When she opened the door to go out, Mr. Jones was standing there.

"Ms. Washington, I need to have a word with you, please."

"Please, come in Mr. Jones. Is everything alright?"

"We have a professional dress code here at the bank, and you don't meet the requirements, so I need you to go home and change, please."

"Of course, Mr. Jones, I'm sorry for my lack of judgment. I'll be back as soon as possible."

"Why don't you take the day off and handle whatever is going on in your life right now. I'll get Tom to handle your workload for today."

"That will not be necessary, Mr. Jones. I'm dealing with things just fine."

"Ms. Washington that was not a request, but a professional way of telling you that your job is hanging in the balance," he said walking out the door.

Feeling ashamed of how this has now affected my job, I picked up my purse and headed out the bank without stopping to let Nancy know what was going on.

"Hello, sexy lady. How about you and me get a room?" some guy said as he was walking by.

"If you don't get out my face with that bull I'll call the police on your ignorant behind!"

"Calm down, little mama, I'm not the one out here advertising all her goods. Have a better day," he said walking way.

"Enough is enough," I shouted out loud.

Getting into my car I made up my mind that it was time to have a real talk with Malachi about where this relationship is going. I pulled up into the driveway to find his car still in the driveway. Getting out I placed my hand on the hood to see if it had been moved, but it was cold to the touch. Giving him the benefit of doubt because of the cut on his hand he may have decided to stay home today. Walking into the house this smell took my breath away causing me to place my hand over my nose. I walked into the living room to find the same mess and more all over the place. He even had that stupid game system still hooked up to the television. Not finding him anywhere downstairs, I went up to see if he was in the house or left with his friend. I heard the shower running so I went into the bathroom to let him know I was home. When I opened the door all the steam had me choking and coughing; he didn't hear it due to the music that was playing loudly. I walked up to the glass shower to open the door. I could already see inside when I placed my hand on the door handle, but it was me that got an eyeful.

"What the hell is this?!" I shouted loudly.

"Sandra, what are you doing home this early?"

"Never mind what I'm doing home early. What the hell are you doing in my shower having sex with my funky behind niece? Keisha, we are supposed to be family, and family don't do this to each other."

"Hello, Auntie Sandra. Would you like to join us?" she said laughing.

"Keisha, I can't believe you would do this to me."

"Get over yourself. Did you really think someone like this could ever fall for the likes of you?"

"I can't stand you and that mouth," I said snatching her out by the hair.

She slipped on the wet floor ending up next to the door. I went to get her but she got up running towards the stairs.

"I'll deal with you when I get back," I said to Malachi before going after her.

"Come back here, Keisha! I'm not done with you yet. You will pay for doing this to me!"

She grabbed her clothes off the living room floor and ran out the front door. I tripped on the beer cans but got back up. Going to the door, I could see her standing in the road trying to put her pants back on which gave me a chance to catch up to her. Jumping off the steps I went after her again.

"Auntie Sandra, stop!" she yelled out.

I stopped in my tracks, but it was too late. The last thing I heard was the sound of screeching tires before falling to the ground.

"Oh my God!! Someone call 9-1-1! Please!"

"I'm so sorry. She came out of nowhere, and I couldn't stop in time."

"This is all my fault for trying to..."

"Trying to what?" the man who hit her said.

"Never mind, just tell them to hurry up and get here."

I looked back over to the house and Malachi was standing in the front door. I motioned for him to come over, but he jumped into his car and left me to answer for this mess.

I could hear the sirens coming in the distance. Every bone in my body was telling me to get out of here, but I couldn't leave family.

They loaded her up then took her to the hospital. I went back into the house to get the rest of my things before driving over. Just as I was about to leave, I noticed her Bible on the dining room table. Looking down at it I still couldn't understand how this book could have such an impact on a person's life. Just when I was about to sit down and open it there was knock at the door.

"I'm Officer Kent. I need to ask you a few questions about the incident, please."

"Yes, let's step outside if you don't mind," I said, so he didn't see the mess in the living room.

"Could you tell me what happened that would cause the victim to run out in front of a car?"

"Her name is Sandra Washington. I was trying to leave, and she tried to stop me is all. It was an accident."

"What kind of argument did you both have?"

"I didn't say we had an argument. You cops always trying to hem someone up to take to jail."

"I'm just trying to take a report on what happened here that's all, but if you need to confess to anything go right ahead."

"I'm done talking to you. If you would leave so I can get back to securing my aunt's home before going to the hospital."

"I think I have everything I need for my report. You have a good evening."

Something told me by his sarcastic remark that I was going to go down for this alone. I need to flip this real quick. Running over to the officer's patrol car, I tapped on the window.

"How can I help you?"

"Officer, if you can come inside the house there is something you should see that could explain what happened."

"Alright, but I don't have time for games," he said getting back out.

We walked back to the front door and I led him into the living room.

"My aunt had a bad fight with her boyfriend who was drunk, and he chased her into the street where she got hit by the car."

"Your earlier statement was that she was trying to keep you from leaving, and the driver said they only saw you standing in the road with her."

"I lied because I didn't want to get involved. He jumped in his car and left before help came. They were always fighting when I came over, and putting his hands on her did not sit well with me either."

"What is this boyfriend's name?"

"She knew him as Malachi Steel, but his real name is Marcus Gregory. I just found out, and came over to warn her that he may be trying to run a scam to get her money."

"This changes my report for sure. I need to go pick this person up for questioning. What is his address?"

"It's 345 Creek Dr. Apt. 5, over in the hood. You may want to be careful because I think he carries a handgun."

"Thank you for coming clean. I need to go now."

He drove off and I went back inside. That will teach Malachi about running off on me.

Chapter 12

Two weeks had passed before I gathered up enough courage to go by the hospital to see my aunt who was still in the ICU. They say she suffered a broken back along with a brain injury when she landed on the ground, which could cause her to not remember things. I walked into her room looking at her chest rise and fall as she was laying there, fighting to live. It suddenly made this the hardest thing in the world. I turned around to leave, but there was an old dude blocking the door.

"I'm Pastor Blake, and you must be Keisha," he said with a smile.

"Wait. How do you know my name, pops?"

"Here let me show you something," he said opening up the Bible he carried in his right hand.

"This is a picture of you and your aunt from when you first moved to Atlanta. You both looked so happy."

"How did you get this picture, old man?"

"She gave it to me when you and she started having trouble and asked me to pray for you."

"Pray for me for what? I don't need that mess."

"Young lady, we all need prayer. Your aunt who is laying there fighting for her life needs it more than ever right now. Even though you had your differences she loves you with all her heart. She even set aside a large inheritance for you in case anything ever happened to her. Her hope was for you to go to college and make something out of your life. Maybe I shouldn't be telling you this, but I wanted you to know how much she loved her family."

"She did this for me? After the way I treated and disrespected her? What God would allow someone to care for somebody like me even if we are family?"

"I want you to read this out loud and then you will have your answer," he said handing me his Bible.

"John 3:16: **_For God so loved the world, that He gave His only begotten son, that_** *whosoever believeth in Him should not perish, but have everlasting life.* You mean to tell me that he allowed his own son to die?"

"Not only did he allow him to die, but he allowed him to suffer for your sins and mine. This is called agape love which is unconditional. It transcends and serves regardless of the circumstance or anything else that life can throw at you. See, Keisha, no matter what happened that got Sister Washington here her love for you is unconditional. The sin we will always dislike, but the sinner we can love and show a better way."

"She has showed me nothing but love since I came here, and all I did was fight her every step of the way, now look at her."

"True, but you can change the outcome to this story if you want to."

"Just how can I do that? Last time I checked I'm not saved like the both of you."

"Here, read this scripture in Matthew 17:20."

"And Jesus said unto them, because of your unbelief: for verily I say unto you, if ye have faith as a grain of mustard seed, ye shall say unto this mountain, remove hence to yonder place; and it shall remove; and nothing shall be impossible unto you. What the heck is a mustard seed anyway?"

"I keep one in my pocket just in case that question comes up when I'm out ministering. This little tiny seed is small in stature, but powerful when activated just like our faith."

"This is tiny. Again, I don't see how this has anything to do with me, old man."

"Do you love your aunt, and are you sorry for what you done to cause what happened?"

"Yes, I'm sorry for what happened to her, and if I could take it back I would."

"Then walk over there and pray for your aunt. The Lord will hear your prayers if your heart is in the right place."

"You want me to pray dressed like this? You must be kidding, right?"

"No, the Lord will hear your prayers for your aunt if they are pure and come from your heart. I need to leave now, but you stay here with her and pray."

He walked over saying a few words to Aunt Sandra who was still not awake before leaving. I pulled up a chair beside her bed making sure not to unplug any of the machines. Taking her hand gently I began to think of what to pray.

Just thinking of all the terrible things I have done to her brought tears to my eyes and all because I wanted revenge. Revenge for her thinking she was better than me for living her life as a Christian. Now look at me about to pray to the same God who she gave her life to. I guess He will humble you in one way or another if you mistreat those who believe in Him. I can safely say that revenge is never the answer if you are planning on taking that route because it never ends with anything good. Well, here goes nothing.

"Lord? Father? God? I'm not sure what to address you as right now. My name is Keisha which you should already have a long file on me up there somewhere. The things I done in my short time on Earth is nothing to brag about either. I didn't interrupt your time to talk about me. I need you to fix my Aunt, Sandra, who is not doing too good right now. If I didn't push her to this point she would not be fighting for her life right now. Yes, I'm confessing to my sins and that I'm the reason for everything. Whatever it takes to fix her I'm willing to do; I'll even give my life to save hers. I just need you to fix this!"

I wasn't sure how to end my prayer because I never prayed before, but I'm hoping He heard my request. Just as I was placing the chair back in place the nurse came in to check her vitals.

"Do they think she is going to pull through?"

"She sure is a fighter I can tell you that. Her faith in the Lord must be strong, and having family praying sure doesn't hurt. Are you a believer?"

"I want to believe there is someone up there watching over this world and that can fix my aunt, but I just don't know how, seeing all the bad things going on around me."

"That is why you have to believe in the Lord, so the evil things of this world don't overtake what is good in it. The Bible says in James 5:16: ***Confess your faults one to another, and pray one for another, that ye may be healed. The effectual fervent prayer of a righteous man availeth much.***"

"I did the praying thing so she's going to be alright now right?"

"Did you confess to her what you did?"

"No I didn't, but what does it matter?"

"Young lady, it matters a great deal. Forgiveness and redemption are the keys that unlock your faith which leads to the impossible becoming possible."

"Let me get this straight, I need to confess to my aunt then find this forgiveness and redemption? I can confess to her right now, but how do I find the other part? I need to go get that preacher dude back for that right?"

"Wrong. People think you need to be in church to give your life to the Lord, but you can accept him wherever you are. A building is not God, but it is a place to come together to worship and fellowship with one another."

"After all I been through and put my aunt through, I'm ready to accept this God into my life."

"Let me ask you this young lady. Are you sick and tired of being sick and tired? Because if not then you will go right back to doing what you been doing in your life. Salvation comes with a price, and the road is not easy, but the rewards and blessings are worth the journey."

"I'm so sick and tired of the life I lead. You have no idea."

"If you would like I can lead you to Christ right here and now."

"I would like that very much because anything is better then what I'm doing right now. Aren't you scared of getting fired and losing your job for doing this?"

"The Lord is my source, and I fear no man when it comes to leading someone to the Lord. I need you to repeat after me if you believe it in your heart to be true. I repent and ask forgiveness for my sins."

"I repent and ask forgiveness for my sins."

"I believe that Jesus is the son of God and that he died on the cross for my sins and was raised from the dead."

"I believe that Jesus is the son of God and that he died on the cross for my sins and was raised from the dead."

"I accept Jesus Christ as my Lord and savior and ask him to come into my life and save my soul."

"I accept Jesus Christ as my Lord and Savior and ask him to come into my life and save my soul."

"That's it, young lady. You just gave your life to the Lord. I still need you to find a church home and get baptized which will be vital to your salvation. How do you feel?"

"Tell you the truth, I don't feel like the same person anymore."

"That is good to hear, and I'm glad I could be here to take part in your new life. I need to get back to work now."

She left and again I went and pulled up the chair next to her bed. This is going to be hard but I know it needs to be done.

"Aunt Sandra, I know you may or may not hear me, but I need to come clean. It was me that set you up with Malachi because I wanted to pull you down to my level and watch your life fall apart. I thought seeing us in the shower would break you completely, but I never wanted it to go this far. I beg and plead for your forgiveness."

I was in tears when I was done. I left the hospital after placing a kiss on the forehead of my aunt. I knew they still didn't have Malachi in custody, so I went over to his apartment to find him. When I pulled up to the building, Blue was hanging around outside of his door which told me he had to be inside.

"Hey, Keisha. What you doing over this way because I don't think he's trying to see you right now."

"Thanks for letting me know he's up there, and I'm sorry for ever treating you badly. I hope you can find it in your heart to forgive me. Here is some money to get something to eat."

"What in the world has gotten into you, Keisha? You have never been this nice to me."

"Jesus Christ, Blue. I got saved and plan to be a better person from now on," I said going up the stairs.

I stood to the side to knock on the door because I didn't know how he would react. I could see him peeking through the blinds.

"Open the door, Marcus!"

"What do you want, Keisha?"

"Marcus, I didn't come over to start any trouble with you. I came to apologize for everything that happened. Can find it in your heart to forgive me?"

He walked back over to the door and opened it. "Ok. What did you do with the real Keisha? I know this can't be happening right now."

"It's me, and this happening. Something happened when I went to visit my aunt at the hospital. Long story short, I gave my life to the Lord and got saved."

"I thought you had to be in a church for that to happen."

"That's what I thought too, but a nurse came into the room and showed me that you can give your life to the Lord wherever you are if you believe. Marcus, I'm telling you that this is the best feeling in the world."

"Well, I'm happy to hear that your life is going better. Now if you would leave I can get back to what I was doing unless you want to go one round for old time's sake."

"Marcus, you're not tired of being tired."

"Keisha, I'm confused about your motives right now. How do you expect me to believe that you can go from being a girl who would curse me out on any given day, to this clean cut person overnight? After all, you're the girl who set me up with her aunt to pull her away from the Lord so you could get revenge.

"Marcus, that is the amazing thing about getting saved; the Lord takes us at our lowest, and transforms us into something better. I know I still have work to do, but I'm going to make it. I just want you to have the same thing too."

"Well, I'm not ready to give up my not-so-good life to follow this God of yours, but thanks for dropping by to share your good news. Please get out because all this rainbow stuff is killing my vibe," he said opening the door.

"Marcus, I don't expect you to change overnight, but I'm not giving up on you so expect to see me around here more from now on."

I left there going by the police station to set things right, then I went back to the hospital. My aunt has a long road ahead, and I plan on being with her every step of the way. When I got to the ICU, the nurse told me she had woken up.

As soon as I walked into the room, my aunt was sitting up in her bed waving for me to come over. My stomach tightened up inside from the fear of how she would react. She reached out her right hand as I got closer which I took with my left hand being careful due to the IV's still attached.

"Aunt Sandra, I'm so sorry for what happened," I said as tears started to run down my face.

"Keisha, please don't cry. I'm just as much to blame for this as you are. When things were going bad with Malachi, I should have ended things and this wouldn't be happing.

"Aunt Sandra, I need to confess something to you that I said earlier while you were asleep."

"Wait. If it's something bad then I don't want you to tell me anything."

"No, I have to do this. I was the one that set you up with Malachi; his real name is Marcus. He was some dude I was sleeping with that would do anything I told him to. I wanted you to suffer to the point that you would leave your faith and wanted to kill yourself. I hated how you thought you were better than me, and acting all holy as if you never done dirt in your life."

"Keisha, I'm so sorry you felt like that. If you would have come to me we could have worked things out. I never wanted anything but the best for you. A man should never come between family unless he is family and it's justified."

"I know now that revenge is never the answer, but I'm thankful for a God of second chances."

"Keisha, what are you talking about? You don't even like church."

"That's the other thing I wanted to tell you, Aunt Sandra. Pastor Blake was here today and we talked about Bible stuff and he showed me things in there that opened my eyes. After he left a nurse came in and she led me to the Lord."

"Are you telling me that you gave your life to the Lord, Keisha?"

"Yes, it has changed my life already in ways I can't describe."

She was so excited about the news she tried to get out of bed.

"Aunt Sandra, you know you can't be out of bed right now," I said helping her back into bed.

"Keisha that is the best news that could have come out of this whole mess. Let's just put all that behind us and move forward."

"Speaking of good news, I have some great news for you, Ms. Washington," a doctor said walking into the room.

"Doctor, I'm ready to hear when I can get out of this place."

"Well, your test results look good. Where we thought your back was broken turns out to be just a mild contusion, and your head injury shows no signs of traumatic brain injury which is good. The best news to come out of this is that you are three weeks pregnant."

"Pregnant! What the hell do you mean I'm three weeks pregnant? That can't be possible because I'm 45 years old, and my ovaries must have turned to dust by now."

"Ms. Washington, I know this must be a shock to you right now, but it is possible to still have babies late in life. I thought this news would brighten things up a little."

"Doctor, the only thing you managed to do is ruin the news of my niece getting saved."

"Well, I see you both have much to talk about, so I will get out your way."

The doctor walked out of the room, and I could see the look of confusion quickly over take Aunt Sandra's face. I myself was in complete unbelief of what just happened. Getting revenge on her didn't include having a baby.

"Aunt Sandra, are you going to be alright?"

"Keisha, give me a second to let this news settle into my spirit because I don't want to say anything that might come out wrong. I can say this, the Lord knows when to save people."

She didn't have to explain what she meant because her eyes told me that if she could come off that bed and get hold of me she would. All I could do at that point was pray to my new

Father in heaven for divine protection and a way out of this room.

"Maybe I should leave you alone for a while and come back later, Aunt Sandra."

"That might be good for the both of us. Hand me my purse out that closet before you go."

Getting her purse I made sure to pat it real good checking for her handgun. I left after that.

Chapter 13

I waited until she was out of the room before pulling out my cell phone.

"Hello, Sandra. How can I help you today?"

"Malachi, or Marcus, whoever you are claiming to be, I just called to tell you that we are having a baby, and I expect you to take care of it!"

"Look, first of all, we are not having anything so there is nothing to talk about. If you are having a problem then I suggest you have it taken care of while you are in the hospital."

"Look, you piece of crap! You are not going to run out on me and your child. If I have to spend every dime I have to take you to court then I will. You hear me talking to you?!"

"I'm sorry about that, but I was playing the game so I didn't hear what you said."

"Don't worry about it. You will hear me soon enough, and that you can count on," I said hanging up on him.

What in the world am I going to do with a baby at my age? I guess this proves that unprotected sex can lead to anything happening, so it's best to wait until marriage with your spouse.

I know one thing, I need to get out of this place right now. Every inch of my body hurt as I tried to get out of bed.

"Ms. Washington, you can't be out of bed right now," the nurse said as she ran into the room.

"Look, I'm leaving this place right now, and no one is going to stop me, understand?"

"You are much too weak to be walking around. Please, let me help you back into bed."

"I told you that I'm leaving this place. Now get out of my way so I can get dressed."

"I'll have to get the doctor if you insist on leaving."

"You do whatever you need to do. It's not going to change anything," I said putting my clothes on.

By the time I had packed up my things the nurse was walking back into the room with the doctor right behind her.

"Ms. Washington, I can't allow you to leave. We are still responsible your wellbeing. Get back into bed, and I will give you something to relax."

"I don't think so, Doctor. Just get me one of the sign yourself out forms, and I'll let you guys off the hook for whatever happens to me. Either way I'm leaving, understand?"

"Calm down, Ms. Washington. Nurse, get the 'against medical advice' forms, and get her to sign them, please. I'm not going to stand here and get you to understand that leaving will put stress on you and your unborn child."

"You just let me worry about this unborn child and my own body," I said sitting down on the bed.

"Look at you, you can't even stand on your own," he said coming towards me.

"Stay back, Doctor!" I shouted putting up my hand.

The nurse came with the paperwork, and after signing them I walked out the room. By the time I got to the elevator my head was spinning. I took a minute to gather myself. When the doors open I turned to see both the nurse and the doctor standing in the hallway watching me. I stepped in and pushed the down button while leaning against the wall so I wouldn't fall.

When it came to a stop, I made my way outside where I had a cab waiting.

"Where are we headed, pretty lady?

"347 Alexandria Dr., and I'm not your baby."

"Sorry about that, Miss. I didn't mean anything. It was just a compliment that's all."

"The last thing I need is a compliment from a man right now. Please, just drive the cab and don't say another word."

I just sat back and let everything replay in my head from the time I met Malachi while still trying to understand how I could be so stupid. They say that love makes you do the dumbest things. Well, I must be this year's poster child.

We pulled up to my house about 20 minutes later. I paid the driver then went into the house. I stayed long enough to change into something more comfortable before heading to the garage to get into my car. Backing out of the driveway, I had one thing and only one thing on my mind at this point.

"Keisha, what is Marcus' address? I need to send him something about the baby."

"It's 345 Creek Dr. Apt. 5. I can come by the hospital to pick it up, and take it over there if you like."

"That won't be necessary because I think you've done enough already. Goodbye, Keisha."

"Wait, don't hang up. What do you mean I done enough?"

I hung up and tossed the phone onto the backseat because I was done with that too. I put the address into my GPS and headed over to confront Marcus for the last time. When I found his place I couldn't believe what I was looking at. Someone staying in a place like this played me for a fool? This proves you can't judge a book by its cover. People need to ask all the questions in the world, and then fact check each and every answer given. I looked around real good before getting out. I made my way up the stairs and located his apartment which wasn't hard from the sound of his video game and him yelling. I knocked on the door with my foot because I didn't know what that was that was running down the door.

"What are you doing here, Sandra?"

"Shut up and get inside," I shouted pulling out my handgun.

"What you plan on doing with that thing? We both know you're soft and don't have the heart to kill nobody."

"Well, that's about to change thanks to you and my niece who you been sleeping with the whole time while playing me for a fool." I said pointing the gun at his chest.

"Wait! I'm sorry for treating you like that, but it wasn't my plan to play you like that. It was all Keisha's idea."

"We are way past the blame game, don't you think, Soon-To-Be-Daddy? I'll be sure to tell your child what a great person you were, and how you wanted nothing but the best for him or her. Now get down on your knees, and say whatever goodbyes you have."

"I don't want to go out like this. Please, let's talk about this. I'm sure we can work things out. Somebody help!!!!"

"You think anybody is going to come running in this neighborhood? They just might thank me for getting rid of the trash in this apartment."

"Sandra, please don't do this!"

"I'm tired of talking. Shut your mouth and look at me. I want you to see your miserable life flash before your eyes," I said putting the butt of the gun up to his forehead.

"Wait!! Don't do it, Aunt Sandra."

"Keisha, don't try and stop me. This lowlife is going to get what he deserves. How did you know I was here?"

"I called the hospital and they said you checked yourself out, and I knew you didn't ask for Marcus's address for anything good."

"Well, you found me. Now get out before I have you join this little farewell party because you did play a role in this also. I guess you're getting what you wanted all along. I'm broken and have stepped away from my faith. Hope you are happy that your little plan worked to perfection."

"I'm not that evil person anymore, remember? Giving my life to the Lord has changed me for the better. I hope you can see that I want things to be better between us. If you pull that trigger and take his life then you are showing me that I made the wrong decision in getting saved."

"I don't know what to believe anymore myself. This piece of trash was supposed to be the man I prayed to God to send me."

"Aunt Sandra, you always told me that going to church is to find the Lord and to fellowship with other believers. You also said... wait I'll read it to you."

"Where did you get my Bible from?"

"I had it since the accident and been reading it day and night. Look, it says right here in Proverbs 18:22: ***Whoso findeth a wife findeth a good thing, and obtained favor of the Lord.*** Now you show me where it says the Lord will send you a man, and I'll leave so you can shoot this man."

"Well, look at my niece getting all religious on me. I didn't think I would live to see this day come. You have changed haven't you, young lady?"

"Yes, the old me wouldn't have even given one thought to come over here to stop you from killing him. But, as a Christian, taking a life is never the answer; neither is revenge. Love and family are the most important things we have."

"That's all you have now. From what I seen being around you, Sandra, is your strong faith in the Lord."

"Shut up, you. What do you even know about faith in the first place?"

"Believe it or not even sinners have faith in what we do. If we didn't we couldn't pull off half the mess we do. The only difference is our faith is not connected to anything. Yours is connected to a God who cares and shows real love and compassion by giving people a chance to change and turn their lives around. Look at Keisha who was once worse than I could have ever been. Now she has a fresh start at having a better life and making it into heaven. That can only come from having the kind of faith that you found at some point in your life."

"You mean to tell me that you saw all that from being around me?"

"Yes I did. Tell you the truth, I never wanted to go through with any of this, but the old Keisha wouldn't let me stop."

"Is he telling me the truth, Keisha or is he just trying to save his own life?"

"He is telling you the whole truth this time. I had to threaten him to get him to do it. He tried to back out many times because he started caring for you."

"You cared about me, Marcus?"

"Yes, I didn't mean any of the things I said on the phone about the baby either. I just got scared about becoming a father because mine walked out on me. If you give me a chance I will prove to you that I can be a great father even if we don't get married."

"I want to trust and believe what you are saying is true, but I just don't know."

"Aunt Sandra, this is where we show love and walk in the faith we say we have."

"Well, Sandra, are you going to shoot me, or are you going to walk in love and faith?"

"I'm going to walk in faith and learn to love you all over again if that works for you both."

"It works for me; how about you, Keisha?"

"I'm in tears right now seeing the power of the Lord work in this apartment. Yes, it works for me too. Now, let's get you back to the hospital."

As we drove over to the hospital, I sat in the back seat with my eyes closed while everything flashed through my mind. When I opened them, Keisha who was driving eyes were looking directly into mine through the rearview mirror. No words at this point were needed because for the first time we completely understood one another. She not only managed to pull me down to where I needed mercy and grace, but I felt everything her young life had been through. Moving my eyes in the direction of where Malachi was sitting, I wasn't sure what the future would be between us. This child growing inside of me would be loved regardless. He didn't give his life to the Lord today, but I could tell he was getting closer. Thank you, Lord, "No Weapon" formed against me will prosper.

Ephesians 4:31-32

Let all bitterness, and wrath, and anger, and clamour, and evil speaking, be put away from you, with all malice: and be ye kind one to another, tenderhearted, forgiving one another, even as God for Christ's sake hath forgiven you.

THE END

Made in the USA
Charleston, SC
11 February 2017